～The～
Silent Witch

MONICA EVERETT

A genius and the youngest mage ever selected to join the Seven Sages of the Kingdom of Ridill. A peerless witch who can omit the chants normally needed when humans use mana. Since she almost never appears in public, her identity remains shrouded in mystery.

SECRETS OF THE
SILENT
WITCH

"Wasting
your talents
as usual,
my fellow
Sage?"

The mountain of papers suddenly flew and danced into the air as though each had a mind of its own, moving from the chair to the desk. To direct each individual document to its respective place elsewhere took very delicate mana control. Seeing her do this as though it were a matter of course—and without a chant, at that—made one of Louis's slender eyebrows twitch.

If they were using this much magecraft by themselves…

then they were some kind of monster.

SECRETS OF THE
SILENT WITCH

I

Matsuri Isora
Illustration by Nanna Fujimi

YEN
ON
New York

SECRETS OF THE SILENT WITCH I

Matsuri Isora

Translation by Alice Prowse
Cover art by Nanna Fujimi

This book is a work of fiction. Names, characters, places, and incidents are the product of the author's imagination or are used fictitiously. Any resemblance to actual events, locales, or persons, living or dead, is coincidental.

SILENT • WITCH Vol.1 CHINMOKU NO MAJO NO KAKUSHIGOTO
©Matsuri Isora, Nanna Fujimi 2021
First published in Japan in 2021 by KADOKAWA CORPORATION, Tokyo.
English translation rights arranged with KADOKAWA CORPORATION, Tokyo, through
TUTTLE-MORI AGENCY, INC., Tokyo.

English translation © 2022 by Yen Press, LLC

Yen On
150 West 30th Street, 19th Floor
New York, NY 10001

Visit us at yenpress.com
facebook.com/yenpress
twitter.com/yenpress
yenpress.tumblr.com
instagram.com/yenpress

First Yen On Edition: July 2022
Edited by Yen On Editorial: Emma McClain, Payton Campbell
Designed by Yen Press Design: Wendy Chan

Yen On is an imprint of Yen Press, LLC.
The Yen On name and logo are trademarks of Yen Press, LLC.

The publisher is not responsible for websites (or their content) that are not owned by the publisher.

Library of Congress Cataloging-in-Publication Data
Names: Isora, Matsuri, author. | Fujimi, Nanna, illustrator. | Prowse, Alice, translator.
Title: Secrets of the Silent Witch / Matsuri Isora ; illustration by Nanna Fujimi ; translation by Alice Prowse.
Other titles: Sairento uicchi. English
Description: First Yen On edition. | New York, NY : Yen On, 2022.
Identifiers: LCCN 2022020923 | ISBN 9781975347802 (v. 1 ; trade paperback) | ISBN 9781975347826
    (v. 2 ; trade paperback) | ISBN 9781975351694 (v. 3 ; trade paperback)
Subjects: CYAC: Fantasy. | Witches—Fiction. | Magic—Fiction. | Bashfulness—Fiction. | LCGFT:
    Fantasy fiction. | Witch fiction. | Light novels.
Classification: LCC PZ7.1.I877 Se 2022 | DDC [Fic]—dc23
LC record available at https://lccn.loc.gov/2022020923

ISBNs: 978-1-9753-4780-2 (paperback)
        978-1-9753-4781-9 (ebook)

10 9 8 7 6 5 4 3 2 1

LSC-C

Printed in the United States of America

Contents

PROLOGUE
The Black Dragon of Worgan

In the Worgan Mountains, in the lands of Count Kerbeck, a dragon had appeared.

The report shook not only the inhabitants of Count Kerbeck's lands but the whole of the Kingdom of Ridill, striking fear into the hearts of all.

Dragons brought disaster. They attacked both people and livestock, occasionally even leveling entire towns. Black dragons, in particular, caused calamities that were the stuff of legends—such a creature had appeared only twice in Ridill's history.

A black dragon's flames were the flames of the underworld itself, capable of incinerating anything and everything. Even if a group of the kingdom's mages was to band together and erect a defensive barrier, those flames would burn up barrier and mage alike. Wherever a black dragon appeared, it was said, the earth would be scorched to ash. Each time one had come in the past, several towns had been wiped off the map, bringing the very kingdom to its knees.

"Lady Isabelle, this mansion is no longer safe. Let us evacuate to the countess's family home."

Isabelle Norton, daughter of Count Kerbeck, shook her head at her maid Agatha's suggestion, a severe expression on her face. "No," she said. "No matter what happens, I shall not leave this place."

Isabelle had only recently turned fifteen. Her bearing and unwavering gaze, however, held the pride and dignity of their noble house, which had protected these lands from dragons for generations.

Dragonraids were the worst here in the eastern reaches of the kingdom, and her family—House Kerbeck—had stood in opposition to the creatures for many years. The history of House Kerbeck was a history of fighting dragons.

In years past, Isabelle had witnessed several disasters borne on their wings. She'd experienced tragedies firsthand. Her family's adoring subjects had seen their crops ravaged and their buildings demolished. Sometimes they lost livestock or even people. She had seen it all—over, and over, and over, and over.

"The knights are fighting on the front lines, and Father is leading them personally. As his daughter, I cannot abandon my own people to flee. It would be dishonorable," declared Isabelle decisively, a slightly sad smile coming over her pretty features as she looked at her maid. "Agatha, thank you for all your long years of service. You are hereby discharged."

"No! No, my lady... I will accompany you to the bitter end."

Isabelle's family weren't the only ones fighting against the dragonraids. Every single person who lived in these lands fought right at the Kerbecks' side. While this girl in her employ was still young herself, she was very brave. Isabelle thanked her maid, nearly crying at the determination she heard in her voice.

If the black dragon was to break through the knights, the lands of House Kerbeck would be reduced to smoldering ashes. But even then, Isabelle planned to remain within the mansion and defend it to her dying breath.

In the absence of her father, the protection of their home fell to her.

"Lady Isabelle! Aggie, you need to hear this!"

Agatha's younger brother, a stable boy named Alan, threw open the door without knocking and burst into the room.

As Isabelle and Agatha prepared for the worst, Alan, cheeks flushed, said, "A mage from the royal capital has slain the black dragon!"

Isabelle couldn't believe what she was hearing.

She was aware that the capital's Dragon Knights, a unit of dragon-slaying experts, had traveled here as reinforcements. She also knew that a single mage had accompanied them—one of the Seven Sages, Ridill's most powerful mages. Her name was...

"It's the Silent Witch!" exclaimed Alan, unable to contain his excitement. "They say the Silent Witch has slain the black dragon all on her own!"

His older sister, Agatha, frowned and reprimanded him. "Alan, you're exaggerating. No mage, no matter how powerful, could ever defeat a black dragon on their own."

"But it's true! The Silent Witch went without the Dragon Knights into the Worgan Mountains and slew the dragon by herself!"

A dragon's scales were extremely hard, and they were highly resistant to mana. They were said to repel average magecraft with ease. To defeat a dragon, one needed to either aim for the spot where its scales were thinnest in the middle of its forehead or go for its eyes. Seeing as dragons could fly, this task was much easier said than done.

Isabelle had heard that even for the Dragon Knights—as skilled and experienced as they were—killing a dragon was far from easy.

And she, thought Isabelle, *did it alone?* Unable to believe this sudden turn of events, Isabelle asked Alan, "...How many casualties?"

"Zero dead, my lady!"

The people Isabelle so loved—every last one of them—had avoided a historic catastrophe and survived. If that wasn't a miracle, what was?

Isabelle let out a cry of relief, overcome with emotion. Just then, Agatha gasped, lifting her head and staring out the window.

"One moment, my lady. That's—"

Isabelle followed Agatha's gaze and spotted something black in the sky. At first, she thought it was a flock of birds, but it quickly grew larger.

When its silhouette came into focus, Isabelle practically heard the blood drain from her whole body. She opened the windows and burst out onto the balcony. Ignoring Agatha's pleas to stop, she grabbed the handrail, leaned out, and looked toward the sky.

"It's... It's a horde of pterodragons..."

Pterodragons were at the bottom of the draconic hierarchy, with low intelligence and no ability to breathe fire. Their mobility and sharp claws, however, still made them a significant threat to humans.

Dragons of this type did not generally form flocks once they reached a certain size, but when a larger and higher-ranking dragon was present nearby, they tended to gather around it and treat it as their leader.

The horde she could see in the sky had probably come to join the black dragon in the Worgan Mountains. And now that it was gone, their coherence had dissolved, and they had bared their fangs, angry with those who had slain their leader.

Isabelle, still leaning over the railing, began counting the pterodragons on her fingers. Once she got to twenty, she took a step back from the railing and stopped.

A dragon's weak points were the middle of its forehead and its eyes. Thus, to get rid of a pterodragon, one first needed to pull it down to the ground. One would then fire a rope from a very large bow, then have cattle drag the rope—and the entrapped dragon—to the ground in order to deliver the finishing blow. Explained like that, it was a simple matter—but eliminating even one required much toil. Often there were casualties.

A horde of more than twenty pterodragons was unprecedented even in House Kerbeck's long history of dragonraids.

Their shrill, deafening cries grew louder as the flock continued to blot out the ashen skies.

"Please come back inside, my lady!"

As Agatha tugged on Isabelle's hand, they felt a strong wind pummel their bodies. It had come from a pterodragon that was nearing the mansion. Isabelle held fast to the balcony's handrail, lest she be blown away.

She had seen it—that dragon's huge eye swiveling to look at her. She let out a soft wail of despair.

* * *

And then a gate swung open in the sky.

A gate of white light had formed in the firmament—bigger than the castle gates, bigger even than the pterodragons. Several glowing magic circles had appeared around it. The doors of the gate had opened silently, letting out a rush of wind from within. That wind carried with it shining white particles that glittered in much the same way as the gate.

It was the sigh of the Springherald, the Shining White Wind—both names for Sheffield, King of the Wind Spirits. Summoning a spirit king was an advanced magecraft technique; only a few in the kingdom could manage it.

Following its caster's command, the spirit king's sigh transformed into sharp spears that pierced through the cloud cover and struck the pterodragons between the eyes.

The dragons had no time to cry out as they were hit. They died without even understanding what had happened. One by one, they fell from the sky.

"This is… They're…"

The giant body of a falling pterodragon was a threat by itself, as it might crush any people or buildings below it. However, once the spears had pierced their foreheads, these pterodragons were enveloped in a glittering wind. They drifted to the ground and piled atop one another like falling leaves.

The spell was hauntingly silent and precise. And standing in front of the pterodragons' remains was the petite figure of the mage who had cast it.

She wore a robe embroidered with gold and a hood pulled far down over her eyes, gripping a staff that was taller than she was. At her feet was a black cat, likely a familiar, nuzzling the hem of her robe.

In the Kingdom of Ridill, the length of a mage's staff indicated their rank. Only seven were permitted to carry a staff longer than they were tall—the Seven Sages. The petite figure who had defeated the pterodragons stood right at the top of Ridill's hierarchy of mages.

She was one of the Seven Sages: the Silent Witch.

"Oh... Wow..."

All the magecraft that Isabelle knew consisted of launching something directly at a target, whether it be flames or wind. It was a wonderful thing, but no more than that.

Never before had she seen a spell as subtle and as beautiful as this one...firing spears so precisely into the pterodragons' foreheads mid-flight before gently, soundlessly setting them down upon the ground.

Isabelle remained on the balcony, her cheeks flushed crimson, and continued to gaze at the miracle their savior had produced.

Meanwhile, a man was watching the same scene from a little ways away.

His blue eyes reflected the figure of the witch who had just cast that quiet, beautiful spell.

He breathed a sigh of admiration and muttered to himself.

"I've finally found it...something that excites me."

His voice was heated, as though he had just fallen in love.

Humans cannot use magic without chanting.

However, there is one girl genius

who has made the impossible possible.

SECRETS OF THE
SILENT✦
WITCH

CHAPTER 1

A Colleague Arrives and Acts Unreasonably

…Squish, squish.

Monica awoke to a soft sensation against her cheek. She'd fallen asleep on her desk, pen still in her hand.

She sluggishly raised her gaze to find herself staring into the golden eyes of a black cat.

The cat had been pushing on her cheek with his paw, and once he realized she'd woken up, his eyes narrowed into a satisfied, human-like grin.

"Hey, Monica. It's morning. Can't sleep forever. What? Are you not going to wake up unless a prince kisses you? *Princess?*"

Unfazed by the talking cat, Monica rubbed her eyes and sat upright.

The black cat was her familiar. Not only could he understand human speech, he could even read. In fact, he was a much more avid reader than she was, taking any free moment he had to do so, nimbly flipping through the pages with his front paws. In particular, he enjoyed adventure novels, and he'd likely gotten the idea of a prince's kiss from one of those.

"…Ugh. Hello, Nero. Is it morning already? …I'm going to go wash my face…"

Monica downed the rest of the cold coffee in her mug, then stood up. Turning her back to Nero, the black cat, she opened the front door and felt a cool breeze tickle her cheeks—a sign of summer's end.

The rickety little house where Monica lived stood on a mountain in the Kingdom of Ridill. There were no other dwellings nearby, and she was more than an hour's walk from the nearest village.

Monica circled behind the house and drew water from the well, a great effort considering her small frame. Recently, great strides had been made in water transportation technology. Pipes had proliferated— not only in major cities but in smaller villages in the area, too. But naturally, none ran to her little hut on the side of the mountain.

Having grown up in the city, she'd found mountain life inconvenient at first. Now, however, she was perfectly accustomed to life in her little house. Best of all, the area was quiet and secluded.

After filling a pail with drinking water, she collected some clothing she'd hung out on a pole to dry and went back inside. Then, as though just remembering, she looked at her reflection in the large mirror in the corner of the room.

An acquaintance had all but forced the mirror on Monica, telling her to put a little more care into her appearance. The mirror itself was very fine and looked out of place in the rickety surroundings.

Its elegant glass reflected a skinny girl with frizzy hair wrapped in a worn-out robe. Though she would be turning seventeen this year, her seedy frame was much paler than it should have been at her age—it was almost the color of a corpse. Her light-brown hair, which she'd haphazardly parted into a pair of braids, was dry and lacked shine, looking even rougher than a bundle of hay. Two round eyes, each framed by dark circles, peeked out from under her bangs, which she'd let grow and grow.

To tell the truth, she looked terrible. She was in no state to be seen by anyone else, but because she spent her time cooped up in a shack in the mountains, such things hardly mattered to her.

Oh, she thought, *but I think today is when my monthly shipment arrives...*

Monica was extremely shy and found it difficult to buy things in stores. Instead, she'd asked the people of the village at the foot of the mountain to deliver food to her.

For a moment, she wavered, wondering if she should re-braid her hair after all. No sooner had she thought this than there was a knock at the door.

"Monica? Your food is here!"

The lively female voice gave Monica a start. She pulled her robe's hood down over her eyes.

In the meantime, Nero jumped nimbly up onto a shelf. "A guest? Guess it's time for me to pretend to be a cat, huh? *Meow*."

"Y-yeah." Nodding to Nero, Monica nervously opened the door.

A wagon was parked outside her house, and next to it stood a girl of about ten. She was a spirited girl, with olive-brown hair tied behind her neck. Her name was Annie, and she was from the nearby village. Usually, it was her job to deliver things to Monica.

Monica peeked from behind the door and, trembling, called out a shaky, "H-hello."

Annie was used to Monica's habits by now, and she pushed her aside, threw the door open, and began lifting the bundles of food.

"I'll bring everything in," said Annie. "Can you hold the door?"

"O-okay…" Monica nodded nervously as Annie skillfully ferried in the goods.

Monica's home had few pieces of furniture, but books and stacks of papers littered the tables and floor, leaving little room to walk. Her bed, of course, had long since been buried under even *more* papers and books. She couldn't even lay down on it. That was why she had lately taken to falling asleep in her chair.

"It's always so messy in here! Are these papers important? Can I throw them out?" asked Annie, suspiciously eyeing the sheaves of paper dominating the floor.

"They—they're all important!"

"Hey, are these formulas? What are you calculating?"

Annie could read, and since she was a craftsperson's daughter, she was also good with numbers. She was only a little over ten years old, but she was smarter than most of the other children her age. But even for her, the rows and columns of numbers on these papers were all but indecipherable.

Monica looked down. Without making eye contact, she answered, "Um, those are…calculations for the, um, orbits of the planets…"

"Oh. What are these ones? Look at all the plant names."

"…Um, those are… I calculated the ratios of plant fertilizers and put them in a table…"

"Then what are these? They kind of look like magical symbols."

"…That's, um, a trial calculation of a new compound magical formula that a professor at Minerva's proposed…" Monica played with the sleeve of her baggy robe as she quietly answered the questions.

Annie's catlike eyes widened. "A magical formula? You can use magecraft, Monica?"

"…I, um, well… Th-that is…," stammered Monica, her eyes drifting left and right.

Nero, who had been pretending to sleep on the shelf, meowed as if to say, *Whoa, are you okay there?*

Monica continued to fiddle with her fingers until Annie eventually gave a light shrug and laughed. "Ha-ha. Of course that's impossible. If you could use magecraft, you'd be working in the capital! Not living like a recluse up here in the mountains."

Magecraft was a means by which one used mana to create miracles. Its techniques had originally been secrets closely guarded by the noble class, but in recent years, commoners had been given more opportunities to study it.

But there were still limitations—one needed significant wealth or talent to enroll in an institution for studying magecraft. For a commoner, becoming a mage was a life-defining success.

If you became a high mage, you might be retained by a noble family, or you could find employment in the Magic Corps, whose members were essentially celebrities.

There was no way Monica, living out here in the mountains, could be a mage—Annie's remark made perfect sense.

"Oh, Monica! Did you hear? Just three months ago, there was a dragonraid near the eastern border."

Monica's shoulders sprang up beneath her robe, and Nero, who had been feigning sleep on the shelf, cracked one eye open. His tail hung down lazily, swaying like the pendulum of a clock.

"I heard some really big pterodragons formed a horde and appeared in a human village! There were more than twenty of them!"

Pterodragons, as their name implied, were dragons with wings. They had lower intelligence and were less fearsome than other dragons but were extremely difficult to deal with in groups. They mostly went after livestock, but starved pterodragons attacking people had become more common in recent years.

"Oh! Oh, and, and! The one leading the pterodragons! It was a legendary black dragon! The infamous Black Dragon of Worgan!"

Dragons whose names specified their color, such as black dragons and red dragons, were of higher rank and seen as a particular threat.

Of those, the black dragon was said to be the *most* dangerous. The unique flames they breathed—blackflames—were flames of anathema. They could mercilessly incinerate even the defensive barriers of high mages. A single attack by a black dragon could easily reduce a kingdom to ashes. Indeed, they were a creature of calamity on an epic scale.

"And! And the Dragon Knights went to slay it, but one of the Seven Sages was with them! Wait, do you know who the Seven Sages are? They're the best mages in the kingdom. Really amazing, you know?"

"Ah, um, I see..."

"The youngest is called the Silent Witch! And they say she beat the black dragon all by herself *and* took down all the pterodragons!"

In countryside villages, these sorts of stories were a precious form of entertainment. Annie's eyes were practically sparkling...but Monica's certainly weren't.

"They say the Silent Witch is the only one in the whole world who can use magecraft without chanting! So magic always needs a chant, right? But not for the Silent Witch! Even without one, she can use powerful magic like *boom, boom, boom!*"

Monica pressed a hand to her stomach in silence. It hurt like it was being squeezed in a vise. Despite the pleasant summer morning, she'd broken out in a full-body sweat.

"I, um, I s-see…," stammered Monica.

Annie put her hands on her cheeks as if enraptured and said, "Oh, I want to meet a real Sage one day! Just once!"

Sevens Sages aside, people out here seldom even saw middle-ranking mages or below. That was probably why Annie found them so fascinating.

Still holding her stinging stomach, Monica took a few silver coins from a leather pouch on the cupboard. It would cover the food she'd had delivered, as well as Annie's tip.

"H-here…," she mumbled, placing the silver coins in Annie's hands and closing her fingers around them. "Thanks, um, for always doing this."

Annie counted the coins, then tilted her head. "I know I ask all the time, but is it really okay to have all this? It's almost twice what the food is worth."

"Y-you delivered it to me, so, um… You can, well, have the rest as pocket money."

Any normal kid would have jumped for joy and tucked the coins away in their pocket, but Annie was a smart girl. She knew the reward went well beyond the work she'd done, and she looked at Monica questioningly. "Hey, what do you do for work, Monica?"

"I, um… Calculations?"

"Are you a math professor?"

"I guess…something…like that. Yeah…"

The documents she had gathered in the house had no real unifying theme. Aside from stellar orbits and fertilizer distributions, they included population totals, tax revenues, shifts in product sales, and various other papers covered in numbers. They lay about the floor in a mishmash that at first appeared like chaos but which conformed to an order and logic only Monica could follow.

Annie seemed decently satisfied with the math-professor explanation.

"Hmm. Then that means the person who came to our village yesterday must be a math professor, too."

"...Huh?"

"He said he was your colleague and wanted to visit you, so I told him the way. He should be here soon."

A colleague. That word was all it took to drain the color from Monica's face.

Trembling terribly inside her baggy robe, she stammered out a question. "Th-that, that person, um, what, er, what kind of, um, person...was he?"

"It was me."

The clear, ringing voice came from behind Monica.

A frightened squeal escaped her throat. With stilted motions, she turned around—a good-looking man with sleek chestnut-colored hair in braids was leaning against the door, a smile on his face. Right next to him stood a beautiful blond woman wearing a maid's uniform.

The man wore a splendid frock coat, with a monocle at his eye and a cane in his hand. Clearly, he was a refined, sophisticated gentleman. Above all, his vaguely feminine, delicate facial features were so attractive, most girls would have been enraptured at first sight.

Monica, however, stared at him in wide-eyed terror, desperately holding back a scream.

"L-L-L-L-L-L-Loui—Louis...?"

"I would appreciate if you wouldn't change my name to L-L-L-Loui-Louis. It's a little silly, don't you think?"

"Ah! I-I'm so s-sorry...," she stammered, on the verge of tears.

Without even a glance in Monica's direction, the man walked straight over to Annie and smiled. Then he took her hand and placed a piece of candy in it. "Thank you for showing me the way, young lady."

"You're welcome."

Annie smiled and returned the handsome guest's show of courtesy, then put the candy in her pocket.

"Anyway," she said, "I don't want to get in the way of your work, so I'll be going now. Bye-bye, Monica. See you again next month!"

The girl waved and left the little house, assuming a more graceful gait than usual. As she listened hopelessly to the clattering of the wagon growing more distant, Monica looked up at the man before her with tears in her eyes.

His frock coat and cane were camouflage. Normally, he wore a gold-embroidered robe and carried a magnificent staff—for he was a mage. The beautiful girl in the maid outfit waiting behind him was no human, either, but a spirit who had formed a contract with him.

"It's, um, good to see you again…Mr. Louis," Monica said, voice shaking.

He put his hand to his breast and offered an elegant bow. "Yes, it has been a while, hasn't it, Lady Monica Everett? Or should I say, the Silent Witch of the Seven Sages?"

* * *

Magecraft refers to the usage of magical power, or *mana*, to cause miracles. Magecraft specifically is a type of magic wherein one chants in order to weave a magical formula and channel one's mana.

Races that excel at using mana, such as spirits, don't need magical formulas or incantations. Humans, however, are unable to control mana without the aid of a chant. They can use a technique called *quick-chanting* to shorten it, but it will still take several seconds.

However, one girl genius had made the impossible possible.

Her name was Monica Everett, and despite her extremely shy nature, difficulty talking, and current status as a mountain hermit, she stood at the pinnacle of Ridill's mage hierarchy. She was one of the Seven Sages—the Silent Witch.

Monica couldn't use *all* the magical formulas currently in existence without chanting, but she could manage it for about 80 percent.

A mage's greatest weakness was being defenseless while chanting. Obviously, on a battlefield, that time could mean the difference between life and death. While some high mages could double the speed of their incantations with quick-chanting, Monica was the only one in the world who required no time at all.

And that was why she'd been chosen as one of the Seven Sages two years prior, at the young age of fourteen.

The story of how this girl genius acquired such an impressive skill was very straightforward.

She suffered from extreme shyness and social anxiety, both of which prevented her from being able to speak clearly around others.

Her reaction to Annie was still relatively minor. With someone she'd never met or someone whose personality clashed with hers, she would become too paralyzed to say anything. At worst, she would throw up or even faint. This obviously presented an obstacle to chanting.

Several years before this, Monica had been attending an institution that fostered new mages. But unable to chant during her practical exams, she'd failed and nearly flunked out. That was when she'd started thinking. With the examiners nearby, she became too nervous to chant—so then, the solution had been to use her magecraft silently.

Normally, a person would have dedicated their efforts to overcoming their shyness or social anxiety. Monica's idea went in an entirely unexpected direction—and most terrifying of all, her talents went on to blossom.

And that was how Monica, for an utterly unmoving reason, mastered the art of unchanted magecraft. From there, her road to the ranks of the Seven Sages had been swift.

Her ability was truly the unexpected gain of a novel, though wholehearted, effort.

* * *

Monica's home in the mountains had only two chairs. One of them currently had a stack of documents on it. She barely ever used that one. Seeing how many papers were in the pile, she gave up on lifting them. Instead, she pointed her finger.

When she did, the mountain of papers suddenly flew and danced into the air as though each had a mind of its own, moving from the chair to the desk.

Producing wind using magecraft wasn't overly difficult. But to direct each individual document to its respective place elsewhere took very delicate mana control. Seeing her do this as though it were a matter of course—and without a chant, at that—made one of Louis's slender eyebrows twitch.

"Wasting your talents as usual, my fellow Sage?"

This man, who had called Monica a colleague, was another of the Seven Sages. He was Louis Miller, the Barrier Mage. He was turning twenty-seven this year, making him ten years older than Monica. They'd both become Sages at the same time, however, so he often referred to her as his "fellow."

When he wasn't talking, Louis appeared to be a beautiful, delicate man, but he was also a martial mage, boasting the second-highest solo-dragon-slaying count in history. He had served as the leader of the Magic Corps and was feared and respected by its members for his shrewdness, or something like that.

What could Mr. Louis want...? O-oh no, is he going to tell me to go slay dragons again?

In any case, he was scary when mad, so Monica gestured him toward the newly cleared-off seat, trembling all the while.

Louis sat down, then looked at the maid waiting behind him. "Ryn, a soundproof barrier, please."

"Right away, sir."

The maid he'd called Ryn gave a nod, and all noise from the surrounding area disappeared at once. The inside and outside of the house had been separated, blocking even the sounds of the wind and the cries of birds.

Ceasing his pretend nap on the shelf, Nero shuddered his whiskers uncomfortably, and his golden eyes stared at the woman in the maid uniform.

She was a tall, slender beauty. But though she had a pretty face, it was expressionless. It made her look somewhat like a doll.

The reason she'd been able to put up a barrier without chanting was that she wasn't a human but a high spirit. Only about ten mages in the kingdom could claim a high spirit as their attendant.

"I'll get right down to it. I've come today to ask a favor of you."

"A...a favor...?" asked Monica without trying to hide her wariness.

Louis offered a graceful smile and rested his chin on his gloved hands. Even his little actions were picture-perfect. "Yes. Last month, I received sealed orders from His Majesty directing me to serve as the second prince's bodyguard."

"...Huh?" Monica's eyes widened.

This kingdom had three princes, each born to a different mother: Prince Lionel, who would be twenty-seven this year; Prince Felix, who would be eighteen; and Prince Albert, who would be fourteen. Viewpoints were split among the kingdom's nobles over which of them would inherit the throne.

Monica had no interest in these sorts of power struggles, so her only knowledge on the matter came from hearsay. Apparently, the first and second princes' factions were about the same size, with the third prince's being somewhat at a disadvantage.

These factions extended to the Seven Sages as well—Louis Miller, the Barrier Mage, was a representative of the first prince's group.

Why would Louis have been ordered to guard the *second* prince? Monica frowned at the disconnect. "U-um, Mr. Louis... You're, um, with the first prince's faction, aren't you?"

"Yes. I have my thoughts as to why His Majesty would order me to guard the *second* prince, but it would be disrespectful of me to speculate on his thoughts. What's important is that he ordered me to carry out my mission without the second prince noticing."

THE BARRIER MAGE
Louis Miller

HIGH WIND SPIRIT
Rynzbelfeid (Ryn)

"…Without, um, the second prince…noticing?"

It went without saying that it was incredibly difficult to guard someone without alerting them. And why would the king order Louis, who supported the first prince, to guard the second? Why did it have to be kept secret from him?

As Monica sank into confusion, Louis continued to explain, his tone detached. "As I said, His Royal Highness Felix is currently attending an elite boarding school called Serendia Academy. If I'm to guard him without attracting his notice… Well, the most appropriate move would be to infiltrate the academy."

Louis, infiltrating a school? In all honesty, Monica couldn't wrap her head around that one. The Barrier Mage—including his appearance—was too well-known. Not to mention his handsome looks would stand out in a crowd. In short, he was particularly ill-suited to infiltration.

Louis seemed to realize this himself. "I could never do it, though," he said plainly. "The academy is under the direct patronage of Duke Clockford, the leader of the second prince's faction. I wouldn't be able to infiltrate it."

As the second prince's maternal grandfather, Duke Clockford had some of the greatest authority in the kingdom. And frankly speaking, he and Louis were like oil and water. It was unlikely that the duke would cooperate with Louis on this secret bodyguard assignment.

"I-if you can't enter the academy…then, um, how are you going to guard him…?"

"That's why I created this magical item."

Louis removed a small, wrapped object from his inside pocket and placed it on the desk. Inside the wrapping was a broken broach. A large crack ran through a sizeable ruby inlaid in the center, and the fine metal clasps had been ruined.

He removed the ruby so Monica could see it. The cracked ruby and exposed setting were each engraved with magical formulas. One look was all Monica needed to understand its basic function.

"…A…a compound barrier? Threat detection, a short-range physical-magical barrier, and a tracking-and-reporting function…?"

"All that from a single glance—but I expected no less. Yes. I took great pains to create this magical item in order to guard the prince."

Magical items were tools using specially tailored jewels and the like imbued with mana to contain a magical formula. They were very convenient, as they granted their benefits even to those who were unable to use magecraft. However, they were still extravagant luxuries owned only by a handful of the most powerful nobles.

And if one of the Seven Sages, the greatest mages in the kingdom, had created this one, it must be priceless. It would probably fetch two or three houses in the royal capital, at least.

Louis brought the cracked ruby up to the light filtering in through the window.

"This is one of a pair of broaches, one ruby and one sapphire. Whoever possesses the ruby will know the location of whoever possesses the sapphire. If the sapphire holder comes under some sort of attack, it will trigger a defensive barrier. When that happens, the ruby will shine in response."

Monica took another look at the magical formula embedded within. She remained silent for a few moments. Then, nervously, she asked Louis, "U-um, so does that mean…it's more for keeping watch on the second prince…than protecting him?"

Louis smiled easily, as if to indicate he had no cause for guilt. "It's only natural a bodyguard would need to know what the person was doing, right?"

"B-but wouldn't he be mad if he found out…?"

"You seem to be somewhat *too* earnest, my fellow Sage… And for that, I offer this old adage." Louis put a hand to his breast, then spoke clearly, like a clergyman citing scripture. "Anything goes as long as nobody knows."

"…"

Is it really that simple? Monica couldn't help wondering. Still, it *would* be difficult to read and understand a formula embedded in a magical item—especially an extremely complicated one made by Louis. Even high-ranking mages wouldn't be able to figure it out so easily.

"I had His Majesty pass the broach to Prince Felix. He was to keep secret the fact that it was a magical item I had created and pretend it was a simple gift from father to son."

As long as the second prince kept the broach on his person, then Louis would be able to constantly track his movements and respond to any emergencies. And besides, Duke Clockford was very strict in his administration of Serendia Academy. Any villains aiming for the prince's life would have a hard time infiltrating it, so there was little chance of anything happening to begin with... Or so Louis had thought.

"Unfortunately, despite working on these broaches for a week without rest, it seems the one His Majesty gave to Prince Felix broke the very next day. A full week with no breaks, and it only took one day... When I saw the ruby crack, it was hilarious. I simply couldn't restrain my laughter. Ha-ha-ha."

Louis's laugh was frighteningly monotone, and his eyes weren't smiling in the least. This was no laughing matter. If Louis's ruby had cracked, that would mean some kind of danger had befallen the second prince.

"S-so...was the second prince...a-all right?"

"Well, when the item broke, I dragged my sleep-deprived body out of bed and ran to the academy right away. And what do you think he said to me?" Louis's eye gave a strange glow from behind his monocle. "His Royal Highness told me that nothing had happened. He told me that he'd broken the broach entirely by accident."

The ruby in Louis's hand made hard, cracking noises. Its shards tumbled out from between his gloved fingers.

"Something I made would not have broken that easily. In fact, I had imbued the broach with several self-protection formulas. Clearly, the blow it took was heavy enough to break them all... Prince Felix, however, isn't talking."

This whole conversation was starting to sound fishy. Monica had a bad feeling about this. A *very* bad feeling.

Louis scattered the ruby's fragments on the desk, then turned a smile on her, which belied his display of brute strength. "You're beginning to get the picture, aren't you?"

Monica shook her head *no* with all her might. Her straw-like braids swished from side to side.

Louis outright ignored her. "I'd like you to infiltrate the academy and protect the prince in my stead."

The way he said it was so very casual, like he was asking to borrow a handkerchief for a second, but what he was asking was no easy feat.

"I—I can't! Wh-why would you want me…?"

"I'm too famous. Look at how beautiful I am. I can't cover all *this* up with a disguise, can I? You, on the other hand, seldom appear in social circles, and you keep your hood down over your eyes even during ceremonies. Nobody knows what you look like. And most importantly…" Louis paused, gave a smile gorgeous enough to enrapture anyone…

"Nobody would ever guess such a plain girl was one of the Seven Sages."

…and insulted her.

From up on the shelf, Nero looked at her as if to say, *Get angry! Tell him off!* But all the weak-hearted Monica could manage was to say "I can't" through sobs and sniffles. "I-I've never, um, guarded anyone before…"

"And that's why you're such a good fit."

"…Huh?" The words surprised Monica enough to make her stop crying.

Louis wearily lowered his gaze and shook his head. "His Royal Highness is an extremely sharp-witted boy… I sent a member of the Magic Corps to guard him, and he saw through it immediately. He's been surrounded by bodyguards for almost as long as he's been alive, so he's good at spotting them. And that's why I'm turning to you."

He then fixed his gaze on Monica and declared, "Even *he* would never suspect a clear amateur, and a little girl at that, was secretly a bodyguard."

"..."

"Above all, you can cast spells silently, without attracting attention. Perfect for a secret bodyguard, wouldn't you say? There is nobody more suited to this mission than you."

Louis's logic *seemed* impeccable, but Monica couldn't help thinking he was just trying to get back at the prince for breaking his magical item.

Seeing that Monica was maintaining her silence, Louis took a deep, exaggerated breath. "It's been about two years since you and I were appointed to the Seven Sages... And the only work you've done has been holing up and staring at papers."

"B-but I went to slay that, um, that dragon, you know, three months ago..."

"I've slain *ten* dragons in the three months since then. What's your point?"

There was no clear hierarchy among the Seven Sages, but Monica and Louis—by virtue of their newness—tended to get assigned a lot of busywork. Over these past two years, Louis had mainly been given dragon-slaying missions and Monica more clerical duties. Most of the documents in her house were related to mathematical work she'd accepted from the other Sages.

"These jobs you're doing are for mathematicians. For bookkeepers. You *do* realize you're one of the seven greatest mages in the Kingdom of Ridill, yes? Doesn't it stand to reason there would be some tasks only you could perform? You do, right? I'm sure you do. If you don't, please understand that, okay? ...I demand it."

An order. How ruthless.

"B-but I only got to join the Seven Sages because I was on the waiting list..."

"His Majesty has left personnel choices for the second prince's guard completely in my hands. In other words...you don't have the right to refuse, my fellow Sage."

Louis grabbed her shoulders and leveled a direct, razor-like glare at her—and out of reflex, Monica nodded. By accident.

He retracted his dangerous smile and let go of her shoulders. "I'm glad we understand each other. In addition, these orders come directly from the king himself...so please consider execution a possibility should you fail, and pay attention."

A shudder ran through Monica at the word *execution*. She didn't want to take on a scary mission like that. Unfortunately, once she had given Louis a nod of agreement, there was no escape. All she could do now was hide her identity at all costs for an entire year, until the second prince graduated, and carry out her mission as a bodyguard.

As she begrudgingly resolved herself, Louis continued smoothly:

"Now let me explain what this mission will actually entail. Several years ago, there was a poor, miserable girl with no relatives living at a certain religious house in Count Kerbeck's domain, in the east of Ridill."

"...Uh-huh."

"But then the previous count Kerbeck's wife, seeing her late husband in the girl, adopted her. The girl was given a happy life, doted on by the previous countess Kerbeck."

"That's a...nice story."

Monica's unsophisticated appraisal prompted Louis to theatrically shake his head. When he continued, his voice was thick with sorrow. "But one day, the countess—an old woman—collapsed from illness and eventually passed on from this world of the living."

"Oh no..."

"Having lost her guardian, the girl was shunned by the others in the count's family and given minor errands as a servant of the count's noble daughter. When that daughter enrolled in Serendia Academy, the poor girl was enrolled as well, as her caretaker."

"I...I feel so bad for her..."

"Indeed. And you will play the part of that poor girl."

Monica was silent for a good ten seconds before opening her mouth to say, "What?"

"That's the story you'll be using to infiltrate Serendia. Make sure you have it good and memorized before your admission."

Monica broke out in a cold sweat. Louis had just assigned her an outrageous backstory, and with complete seriousness.

"Um...," she mumbled. "I-it's so much, I can't even..."

"As long as you have a troubled past, nobody will pry very much. Incidentally, I based your story on a character from this book."

Ryn, the high-ranking spirit wearing a maid outfit and waiting behind Louis, smoothly produced a book. The author's name was Dustin Gunther—a recent favorite novelist of Nero's. With cultivated motions, Ryn held the book out to Monica and spoke.

"It is a romantic novel where the heroine, bullied by the count's daughter, catches the eye of a prince. Eventually, the two fall into a forbidden love. The dismal and knavish methods by which the noble daughter bullies her are written very intricately. It is, in my opinion, a fascinating work."

Nero listened to Ryn's description from atop the shelf, a look of keen interest on his face, his tail swaying to and fro. This house contained several books by Dustin Gunther, but they were all older ones. The book Ryn had was the author's newest work. It was only natural that Nero would be interested.

With Monica flustered, Ryn gently placed the book into her hands. "I will lend this to you. I hope it serves you well as a reference."

How is this supposed to be a reference? And for what? thought Monica, pretending to flip through the pages. She'd spent many hours reading magecraft-related books, but she wasn't too familiar with novels meant for entertainment, and the contents didn't stick well in her mind.

"U-um... The story you thought of, Louis—it means I'll enroll along with Count Kerbeck's daughter, but..."

"Yes, of course! I've already told Count Kerbeck about it and asked Lady Isabelle, his only daughter, to provide assistance."

Monica's eyes widened. "W-with a story like *that*?! W-won't that, um, cause trouble for the, um, House of Kerbeck?" After all, if they followed Louis's story, that would make Count Kerbeck and his daughter, Isabelle, out to be the bad guys. She paled. She couldn't possibly make them do such a thing.

Louis, however, was calm and relaxed. "What do you know about Count Kerbeck?"

"Huh? Um..."

Monica was good with numbers, but not so much with remembering the names of people and places. Still, the name *Count Kerbeck* did tug at her memories a bit. She recalled hearing it relatively recently.

"Oh... The dragons..."

"Exactly. When you slew the Black Dragon of Worgan three months ago, that was in Count Kerbeck's lands. He is deeply grateful to you for it—in fact, he said he would assist the Silent Witch with anything."

Count Kerbeck had prepared a feast of gratitude for Monica, who had slain the Black Dragon of Worgan. However, Monica had declined and fled back to her cabin, so she'd never met the count *or* his daughter.

Monica had been worried that her refusal would have soured the count's opinion of her, but apparently, he'd been impressed—he'd taken it as a show of the Silent Witch's profound modesty.

"I've already given the cover story to Count Kerbeck and his noble daughter. The count was more than happy to oblige. 'Well now! That sounds just like a ballad, doesn't it?' he said."

"M-more than happy...?"

"And Lady Isabelle's eyes were glittering. 'Villainesses are all the rage lately!' she said."

"A-are they...?"

Apparently, the novel Louis had drawn from was hugely popular in the capital. As it turned out, Lady Isabelle was a big fan, and she'd make special trips for each new book.

"Lady Isabelle is hard at work developing her character into the perfect villainess to bully you."

"..."

"Essentially, it comes down to this. You will infiltrate the academy, Lady Isabelle will bully you, and you will protect the second prince. What? You're great at playing the bullied child, aren't you?"

"…" Monica couldn't even answer that one…

…because she was nearly unconscious.

If he had already arranged Count Kerbeck's assistance in the matter, Louis had *never* intended to let Monica out of this.

* * *

Even after Louis and Ryn left her cabin, Monica remained in a dazed state on the floor. Louis had said he would come by at the same time the next day and that she should have her things ready to go by then. But she honestly didn't even know where to start.

"Hey, Monica. Are you alive? Heeey!"

Nero used his front paw to prod Monica's foot. Normally, the soft, squishy pad was a soothing sensation for her, but she couldn't enjoy it right now.

"What do I do…? I—I can't guard someone… I was only on the waiting list for the Seven Sages…"

"You said that before, didn't you? What do you mean by 'waiting list'?"

Nero was confused—he didn't know much about human affairs. Sniffling loudly, Monica recalled the Seven Sage examinations two years ago.

"T-two years ago," she began, "they were selecting new Sages…"

"Right."

"…And I… During the interview, I was so nervous that I began hyperventilating."

"Right."

"…I don't remember much, but they said my eyes rolled back, and I fainted. I was foaming at the mouth…"

Nero, eyes narrowed, wagged his tail. "…And how on earth did that get you into the Seven Sages?"

"I-it just so happened that one of the Sages at the time fell ill and had to quit...so a second spot opened up. And then they chose me out of pity..."

Nobody had told her this, but Monica was sure that Louis had been the only person who had actually passed the examination. He was a talented mage. Former leader of the Magic Corps, he backed up his accomplishments with his incredible abilities. Monica, on the other hand, was a little girl who was only good at calculations, who stayed holed up in a laboratory year-round. There was no comparison.

"I can't believe he'd choose someone from a waiting list as a bodyguard for a prince... I—I can't do it! I can't, I can't!"

As Monica hung her head and buried her face in her hands, Nero patted Monica's foot soothingly. "If you really don't want to do it, why not just run away?"

"I—I can't. Because if I run away...Louis will chase me to the ends of the earth..."

Louis Miller, the Barrier Mage, was a beautiful man with the manners of a noble—but he was also one of the most powerful martial mages in the kingdom. Monica knew that underneath those gloves were hands heavily calloused from fighting.

"Is that guy even *human*? He seems more like a keeper of the *underworld* than one of the Seven Sages."

"He's about as scary as one!"

Monica knew that she couldn't run, but she was still scared. As she sniffled again, Nero, tail swaying, made a proposal.

"In that case, let's be positive about it, eh? You're going to be guarding a prince. You know, a prince! They're really cool, right? They practically sparkle. Human females all love princes, don't they?"

"...I don't know."

"The Seven Sages have to do ceremonies and such, yeah? Have you ever seen a prince's face before?"

Monica shook her head. With her social anxiety, Monica hated crowds. During ceremonies, she always had her robe's hood pulled deep over her eyes and kept to herself until it was over with. She'd never even gotten a good look at the king's face up on his throne.

"Hey, Monica. I just had a thought."

"…Hmm?"

"If you don't know what the person you're guarding looks like… isn't that bad?"

"…What should I do…?"

She couldn't possibly be honest with Louis and tell him she didn't know what the second prince looked like. Not to mention the punishment for failing this mission was…

The word *execution* flew around in her mind, causing her to fall face-first on the floor and break down in tears. Nero patted her knee with his front paw to try and offer some degree of consolation.

CHAPTER 2

The Villainess Is Fond of the Silent Witch

Every child in the Kingdom of Ridill knew the nursery rhyme "Old Man Sam's Pigs."

> *Old Man Sam raised many pigs.*
> *In the first winter, he sold one*
> *In the second winter, he sold one*
> *In the third winter, he sold two*
> *In the fourth winter, he sold three*
> *In the fifth winter, he sold four*
> *As the wagon's wheels went clatter-clatter*
> *The little pigs cried oink-oink*
> *If in the sixth winter he sold eight pigs*
> *How many did he sell in the tenth winter?*

Monica was currently on her way to Louis's estate in the royal capital, but her mind was completely taken up by "Old Man Sam's Pigs"—specifically, how many pigs were being sold.

If the answer to the song's riddle is the sum of the two previous years, then on the tenth year, he'd sell fifty-five... On the eleventh, eighty-four, and on the twelfth...

In her head, mostly as a way to escape reality, she continued to calculate the numbers of pigs at length. When she reached 10,946 pigs, Louis, who was sitting next to her, said, "You don't look well, my fellow Sage."

"...and on the twenty-eighth, it would be 317,811 pigs, on the twenty-ninth it would be 514,229 pigs..."

"Hello? My fellow Sage?"

Louis poked her, finally yanking her from the fast-proliferating pig farm and back into reality.

"I-I'm sorry! I was just, um, thinking about things..."

"Thinking about things?"

Monica fell silent, not able to admit she was calculating the number of pigs to be shipped.

At the moment, they were flying through the air using wind magic provided by Ryn, the spirit bound to Louis. Flight magic was extremely difficult and used up a lot of mana. Even a high mage would run out of steam after about thirty minutes.

Ryn, however, was a spirit, meaning she could pull off the feat of high-speed movement up in the air. She'd enclosed Louis, Monica, and even Nero—who had slipped into the baggage—in a hemispherical wind field. As a spirit, she possessed far more mana than humans, and her talent for using it meant she didn't need to chant.

Whenever she witnessed how amazing spirits were, Monica was reminded that her own ability to use magecraft without chanting wasn't that incredible in the grand scheme of things. People admired and complimented her for it only because she was a human.

Miss Ryn is amazing, but so is Mr. Louis for having a contract with her...

Monica, in the meantime, was just a shut-in researcher whose only strong point was being able to cast spells a little more quickly. *And yet, he wants* me *to guard royalty...*, she thought, gripping the travel bag containing Nero and hanging her head.

Just then, Ryn, who was in front of them maintaining the field, adjusted her head so that she could see Louis and Monica without turning her body. The motion was like that of a doll with a broken neck. It shocked Monica, but the pretty maid's expression remained impassive—which only made her look like even *more* like a doll.

"We will be arriving soon," she announced. "To that end, I have a proposition for a completely unprecedented landing method—"

"That is quite fine. Please take us down safely."

Ryn remained straight-faced, but her response sounded somehow disappointed.

"Of course, sir."

Once they'd entered a residential area, she set them down gently, as ordered.

Louis's mansion was relatively cozy but neat and trim. Monica had initially assumed it would be more extravagant; its surprising homeliness took her off guard.

"Welcome to my humble abode," said Louis, opening the door. Inside, Monica could see a woman who looked to be in her midtwenties. Louis's face immediately broke into a smile. "I'm home, Rosalie."

His tone was quite lively. The woman must have been his wife—Rosalie Miller.

Compared with the elegance of Louis's appearance and dress, she was a little plainer. She wore clothing without much ornamentation but in a style that allowed freedom of movement. Her brown hair was bundled together behind her head.

Louis's body language indicated that he'd missed his wife a lot, but Rosalie's attitude was indifferent. Instead, she stared unsmiling at Monica as Monica hid behind him.

She isn't angry that her husband brought a young girl home without any warning, is she? Monica thought. Uneasy, she lowered her gaze to try and flee from Rosalie's, but the woman quickly walked over, grabbed Monica's cheeks in her hands, and turned her face upward.

"Eek?!"

"Excuse me for a moment."

As Monica stiffened in terror, Rosalie brushed back her bangs and tugged on her lower eyelids.

"U-um, I, wh-what—?" stammered Monica.

"Hold still," ordered Rosalie. "Now open your mouth wide."

Monica did as she was told. Rosalie checked her oral cavity. Then she checked every other part of her body, even down to her hands and nails.

"Eye movement normal, no gingivitis. Insides of the lower eyelids are white, and the nails are whitish as well. Dry skin, too... Malnutrition, plus signs of anemia. How old are you?"

With Rosalie's serious expression right in front of her, Monica—half crying at this point—answered in a shaky voice, "I-I'll be, um, seventeen this year..."

"And too thin for your age. What do you normally eat? Average daily sleep time?"

"It, um, varies a lot, I guess..."

The more questions Monica answered, the severer Rosalie's expression became. After a few more rounds, Louis looked at his wife, seeming like he really wanted her to give him some attention. "Rosalie," he said, "your new husband has come home. Won't you give him a kiss and welcome him back?"

"The patient is of utmost importance," said Rosalie, swiftly cutting down the suggestion.

"I'm...healthy...," Monica insisted, almost inaudible.

Rosalie shook her head and declared, "I don't know who you are or where you're from, but it doesn't take a doctor to see that you're a living, breathing example of *un*healthiness. My prognosis is to get plenty of food and rest. I also suggest taking a bath and changing out of those clothes."

There was no doubt this was Louis's wife. There were many differences between the two, but their outspoken, direct manner of communication was exactly the same.

As Monica's mouth flapped open and closed without making any sound, Louis shrugged in resignation.

"Rosalie is a doctor. You may want to follow her instructions—for your own good, my fellow Sage."

* * *

After being shoved into the bath by Rosalie Miller and given a warm meal and a change of clothes, Monica finally had a chance to breathe on her way to the mansion's guest room. On the way there, Nero poked his head out of her bag—he'd been in there for the entire trip. But when Louis entered the room, he immediately ducked back inside.

With an uninterested glance at Nero, Louis said, "Rosalie insists that you need to take a nap, but before that, I must introduce you to our guest, who will be arriving shortly."

"G-guest?" Monica tensed.

Louis nodded, then gave the name. "Count Kerbeck's daughter, Lady Isabelle Norton."

Lady Isabelle was Monica's coconspirator for this mission and would be enrolling in Serendia Academy with her. *He's right*, thought Monica. *It's probably a good idea to see her before we go to school.*

Then something occurred to her.

"U-um, is 'Kerbeck' not her family name?"

"I'm sorry?"

Louis looked like he didn't understand the question. Monica played with her fingers and said, "Um, well, she's the noble daughter of Count Kerbeck, so I assumed her name would be Isabelle Kerbeck..."

"Kerbeck is their peerage title. Most nobles ranked count or above are called by a peerage title."

"...?"

With Monica seeming baffled, Louis's expression stiffened, and his cheeks twitched. "My fellow Sage, how much do you know about the noble ranks?"

Monica simply shook her head. The smile finally disappeared from Louis's face.

"You surely *can* name our kingdom's ranks from highest to lowest, yes?"

"...B-baron, marquess, duke, count?"

At her confused response, Louis put on a magnificent smile that definitely said, *You're an idiot, girl*. "Not a single one of those was in the correct position, and you've entirely forgotten about viscounts."

"...Eep!"

"For someone who knows all one-hundred-plus magicule names, how can you not remember *five* noble ranks?"

All she could say was that she'd never been interested. But if she was that blunt, he was sure to start hurling insults, so she just looked down in silence.

Louis pushed his monocle up with a fingertip and heaved a sigh. "First, try to get at least this into your head. In Ridill, the noble ranks are, from highest to lowest, duke, then marquess, then count, then viscount, then baron. There are other ranks below that for the lesser nobility, but I'll spare you the details. For now, just remember that if you ever meet someone who is a duke or duchess, that means they're most likely part of the royal bloodline."

Committing his words to memory, Monica muttered, "C-counts are higher than I expected." To tell the truth, she'd thought count was the *lowest* rank.

Louis's eyes widened until they couldn't widen any more, staring at her in disbelief. "...My fellow Sage? You *do* remember that you have a noble rank yourself, yes?"

The Seven Sages were given a special rank called a "count of magic" that corresponded to a normal count. In other words, Monica was a noble, too.

She was also a rare female titleholder, one of less than ten in the whole kingdom...but for someone who had been shut away in a mountain cabin for two years, she certainly didn't think of herself as a noble.

Now that she thought back on it, she *did* remember receiving a bunch of things when she'd become one of the Seven Sages, like a certificate of noble rank and a ring. She'd forgotten where she'd put them. They were probably buried somewhere in the stacks of paper in her cabin.

When Monica confessed to this, Louis frowned, put his fingers together, and sighed.

Then they heard a knock at the door. Ryn's voice came from outside. "The young lady of Count Kerbeck has arrived."

Louis gave Monica a glance and said, "Let's get going."

Monica, holding her aching stomach, wobbled to her feet.

* * *

"Ohhh-ho-ho-ho-ho! Good day to you!"

A high-pitched laugh rang out, probably audible from anywhere in the mansion. Its source was the one Monica had gone to meet—a girl who was about the same age as she was. She wore a scarlet dress with extravagant embroidery. Her brightly colored hair, which had a hint of orange in it, was full of splendid curls.

Monica stood before the door, completely in awe. The lady Isabelle Norton, daughter of Count Kerbeck, brought a folding fan to her lips and narrowed her eyes at Monica in a wicked expression.

"Oh, well, hello there, *Auntie* Monica. Thin and seedy looking as always, I see. To think your name besmirches the family register of House Kerbeck—why, it absolutely *shames* me!"

Even though Monica didn't understand what she was talking about, the clear hostility in the girl's voice stung. Weak-willed as she was, she was very sensitive to when others had it out for her. She was so timid that even the tiniest thorns would cause her to wither.

And now that Isabelle had made her malice clear, tears immediately began to form in her eyes.

But before she curled up on the spot, Isabelle's mean-spirited expression withdrew, replaced by a charming smile. "How was it? Did that not sound exactly like a villainess? I've been practicing that voice every single day since receiving this duty! I am confident that the sharpness of my laugh outstrips all competitors!"

Can a laugh be sharp? What is she talking about? Monica's eyes went wide in puzzlement.

Isabelle seemed to snap out of it and remember something. "Oh, dear me. How callous of me not to introduce myself." She picked up the hem of her dress and gave an elegant curtsy befitting a beautiful maiden. "It's a pleasure to make your acquaintance, Lady Monica

Everett, the Silent Witch. I am Isabelle Norton, daughter of Azure Norton, Count Kerbeck. You did us a great service in slaying the black dragon. On behalf of my father and our people, I extend to you our greatest thanks."

As Monica stood there, still as a statue from shock, Isabelle smiled at her. It was an incredibly cute—and most importantly friendly—smile, and none of her previous nastiness could be seen in it.

"Ah, to think the Sage who defeated the fearsome Black Dragon of Worgan and tore that horde of pterodragons from the sky would be such an adorable person! Why, when I asked your age, I was told you and I were but a single year apart!"

If we're one year apart, that would make her eighteen this year, thought Monica in a corner of her paralyzed mind.

Meanwhile, Isabelle took her hand, her cheeks flushing a rosy pink. "Oh, please…Would you permit me to call you my elder sister, Monica?"

But as it turned out, she was actually younger.

"Ah, I, um, well…"

With Monica flustered, Louis, who had been watching their exchange with a grin from his seat on the sofa, put in, "My fellow Sage, why don't you greet Lady Isabelle and thank her for offering her assistance?"

"I… Pleased…to, um, m-meet…youph," stammered Monica, her breath half caught in her throat.

Louis shrugged in resignation. "I'm terribly sorry, Lady Isabelle. The Silent Witch is a rather shy sort, you see."

"No, no, I don't mind it at all. My sister may be shy, but…I know she's gallant and stronger than anyone!"

Who on earth is she talking about? thought Monica. *I'm hardly strong. And I'm definitely not "gallant."*

But Isabelle was lost in her own little world. When she spoke, it was in a rapture, with her hands at her rose-colored cheeks. "It was said that even the Dragon Knights would have had a difficult time slaying the Black Dragon of Worgan. The flames it breathes are the flames of the underworld. They can even incinerate magic barriers! It's the strongest, wickedest dragon of them all! And, oh, to slay it all by oneself—that isn't something just anyone could do! And on top of all that, you left without a word after doing the deed... It's... It's just... It was so cool!"

"Um... I, well..."

The only reason Monica had participated in the slaying of the black dragon at all was because Louis had all but dragged her out of her mountain cabin, saying, "Why not get some exercise once in a while?" She'd declined to take part in the feast not out of modesty but out of shyness.

But to Isabelle, who knew none of that, Monica evidently appeared like a gallant, humble, powerful mage. It was a massive misunderstanding, but Monica wasn't eloquent enough to explain all that.

And as for Louis—*he* was trying to take as much advantage of the situation as he could.

"My sister! I have heard of your task to infiltrate Serendia Academy in order to guard Prince Felix! I consider it the highest honor to be able to assist you in this matter! I will torment, frustrate, and excruciate you so much that nobody will ever suspect you! That way, you can focus on guarding His Royal Highness without worrying about a thing!"

When she was finished, Isabelle took Monica's hand and shook it fiercely.

Monica, who couldn't do anything but let the current carry her along, only managed to nod.

CHAPTER 3
How Quickly the Headmaster Rubs His Hands

Serendia Academy was named for Serendine—the Goddess of Light and one of the Spirit Kings—in order to receive her divine protection. Her staff and crown of lilies served as the motifs for the school's emblem.

Originally, it was not the custom of royalty and nobility to send their children to school. As the times progressed, however, more and more noble children began attending educational institutions. Serendia Academy was one such place.

Now there were many schools, including boarding schools and schools for girls, but Serendia Academy held the honor of being the first school attended by a member of Ridill's royalty.

The Kingdom of Ridill had three elite schools in particular: Serendia Academy, where members of the royal family went; Minerva's Mage Training Institution; and the Temple-Affiliated University.

Among them, the University was most focused on law. Minerva's areas of expertise were magic and magecraft. Serendia Academy, in the meantime, excelled in teaching all subjects besides those two.

The academy had it all: first-rate instructors, an enormous collection of books, and facilities and equipment befitting its noble-born students.

Getting into the academy required a substantial enrollment fee and donation, but students had a tremendous advantage finding work in the court after graduation. Among nobles, being able to call yourself a Serendia Academy alumnus was a status symbol.

It hardly needed to be said that those who had participated in the academy's student council were viewed with particular awe. Especially with the second prince, Felix Arc Ridill, currently serving as the council's president, becoming a member meant a chance to be chosen as his close aide.

Indeed—normally, becoming a student council member would guarantee a secure future.

...So then why is this happening?! Aaron O'Brien cried out in his mind. Aaron was the current student council accountant at Serendia Academy.

He stood in the center of the room, with the rest of the student council surrounding him. They'd been his fellows until just the previous day, but now, they all looked at him as though he was a criminal.

Tension filled the student council room, but one person was smiling: a young man sitting in the president's chair with a fist to his cheek—the student council president and second prince of the Kingdom of Ridill, Felix Arc Ridill.

"Now then."

Two words from Felix were enough to completely change the mood. Aaron's shoulders sprang up. Felix directed a smile at him— the smile of a deeply compassionate saint.

"Our investigation has uncovered traces of tampering," began Felix. "Specifically, a misappropriation of budget funds. And it happened more than just once or twice... Isn't that right?"

His voice was gentle and exceedingly calm, yet so cold that it felt like a knife stabbing into the listener's heart.

Aaron remained silent. The secretary, a young man with brown hair and slightly droopy eyes named Elliott Howard, leveled a sharp gaze on him.

"Then you've lost count of how many times you misappropriated funds?" he said. "...Because just from what I've found, the count is more than thirty."

Elliott's tone was flippant, but his eyes were replete with disdain as he watched Aaron.

After Elliott, another secretary—a beautiful blond girl named Bridget Greyham—covered her mouth with a folding fan and remarked, "That is quite a lot, considering it covers only last year's general budget. But did he not *also* embezzle funds from the special budget?"

At Bridget's words, a short boy with bright brown hair named Neil Clay Maywood—their officer of general affairs—nodded. "Yes. We're still reviewing the special budget, but there were signs of falsification there as well, so there is little doubt. A preliminary count places the combined total at…close to fifty instances."

Faced with one person after another pointing out his misdeeds, Aaron clicked his tongue. *How the hell am I supposed to remember how many times I did it?!* His collaborator had warned him he was going overboard, but even so, he should never have been discovered.

As Aaron maintained his silence, Felix, gentle smile still on his face, began again. "We selected you for the student council at the recommendation of my grandfather, Duke Clockford."

Student council members were appointed by the president. There had been several who had used money in order to curry favor with Felix, and by extension with his grandfather, Duke Clockford. One of those who had offered quite a lot was Aaron's father, Count Steil.

That was why Duke Clockford had ordered his grandson Felix to select Aaron for the student council. If he'd only done his job as accountant properly, both his and Count Steil's futures would have been secured.

Unfortunately, House Steil had contributed a little too much to Duke Clockford, resulting in near-destitution. As a result, Aaron's allowance had been greatly reduced, and he had started embezzling student council funds for money to fool around with.

Damn it, damn it, damn it…!

Aaron ground his teeth and Felix's eyes narrowed. As the prince passed his judgment, his voice was incredibly soft and ice-cold. He meant to corner Aaron slowly and prolong his torment.

"I cannot levy any punishment greater than expulsion. However, my grandfather will likely cut all ties with Count Steil."

SERENDIA ACADEMY
STUDENT COUNCIL SECRETARY
Elliott Howard

SERENDIA ACADEMY
STUDENT COUNCIL VICE PRESIDENT
Cyril Ashley

SERENDIA ACADEMY
STUDENT COUNCIL SECRETARY
Bridget Greyham

SERENDIA ACADEMY STUDENT COUNCIL
OFFICER OF GENERAL AFFAIRS
Neil Clay Maywood

SECOND PRINCE OF THE KINGDOM OF RIDILL
SERENDIA ACADEMY STUDENT COUNCIL PRESIDENT
Felix Arc Ridill

Aaron felt the blood drain from his body. Everyone who studied at this academy knew that behind the second prince was the most influential noble in the kingdom: Duke Clockford. And the duke was a coldhearted, merciless, and brutal man.

"It would seem your father sought the trust of House Clockford in order to obtain loans. Oh, how sad. After this, Count Steil will be unable to receive a loan from anyone, and your house will likely fall into ruin."

Aaron's face became slick with sweat. *I'll be fine*, he thought. *I know it. I know they'll do something about this!*

He'd had a collaborator this whole time. He was certain they would pull some strings and get him out of this mess.

Yes... Erm, they'll, um...

But when he tried to envision his collaborator's face, he found that he couldn't. At first, he thought it was only confusion due to his current distress, but the more he tried to remember, the more blurred his memories became. His thoughts dulled. His head swam.

Why? Why can't I remember them?

Aaron O'Brien had had a collaborator. He was sure of it. Pretty sure, at least. They had conspired with him in exchange for half the takings.

And yet, he couldn't remember that collaborator's face, or their voice, or their name—nothing at all.

"Ah, ah, ahhh..."

For some reason beyond his understanding, the memory had completely vanished. The sensation was similar to the fear one might feel seeing a gaping hole in one's body.

Face soaked with sweat, he held his stinging head and began to tremble uncontrollably. His intense fear gave way to panic. Aaron was a breath away from losing it—and then Felix, with that saintly smile, delivered the finishing blow.

"...Do you understand? Your foolishness has caused the down-fall of House Steil."

Aaron could hear a thread snap in the back of his mind. He had lost control.

The inside of his head was hot. Really hot. It felt like the blood vessels were being burned away—and he gave himself up to the heat, shouting out as froth began to form on his lips.

"Shut up, shut up, shut up! The royal family are just…just lap-dogs of the duke!"

With all his self-control gone, Aaron jumped onto the desk in a rage and tried to grab Felix. Before he could touch the prince, however, one of Felix's aides waiting at the wall leaped into action and restrained him. This young man with platinum-blond hair was Cyril Ashley, the student council's vice president.

Cyril swiftly chanted a spell, then gave the command: "Freeze!" Immediately, Aaron's feet were covered in blocks of ice.

Now that he'd restrained Aaron with ice magic, Cyril's well-defined features warped into an angry glare. "How *dare* you! Brutish remarks *and* violence directed at His Royal Highness… You deserve to die a thousand deaths! I'll turn you into an ice sculpture and knock you out the window!"

The ice covering Aaron's feet began to make cracking noises as it crawled up each of his legs. At this rate, he *would* transform into a full-body ice sculpture.

But as the ice reached Aaron's knees, Felix interrupted.

"It isn't your job to deal with him, Cyril."

At Felix's command, Cyril immediately halted the progress of his spell. Then he bowed his head to the prince.

"… I acted out of line, sir. Please accept my humblest apologies."

"You were concerned for my safety, right? Thank you for protecting me." Felix smiled at Cyril before letting his gaze drift back to Aaron.

His eyes, sky blue with just a drop of green mixed in, looked mercilessly upon Aaron.

"Aaron O'Brien, you shall confine yourself to your dorm until official notification of your expulsion is handed down. You should have plenty of time to reflect on how much of an idiot you must be to have been outwitted by a lapdog of the duke."

"Ugh," muttered Aaron from trembling lips.

His memories were rapidly growing hazier and hazier. He *knew* he'd had a collaborator. He was sure of it, but he couldn't remember... No, no, no.

...Had he really been working alone?

* * *

In the carriage heading for Serendia Academy, Monica was at a loss.

"Wh-what to do, what to do...?"

To be precise, the reason she was cradling her head in her hands at the moment had to do with the rooms in the girls' dormitories.

Serendia Academy was a boarding school, and its dorm assignments were generally two people to a room. But Monica, who had been living in a mountain cabin due to her fear of being around people, was never going to survive living in a two-person room.

As if having to guard the prince isn't troublesome enough!

"It doesn't need to be anything fancy... Just please let me have an attic room..."

The school did have single-person rooms, but those were apparently limited to students with exceptional grades or those who had made significant donations. To tell the truth, it wouldn't have been that difficult to pay the required donation. Monica had barely touched the income she received as one of the Seven Sages, so money wasn't the issue.

But with her cover story as Monica Norton, the outcast of House Kerbeck, it would no doubt arouse suspicion if she paid a large donation to secure a single room.

The problem would be solved were she to share a room with her collaborator for this mission, Isabelle, but the younger girl was a first-year in the advanced course. The dorms usually put people of the same year together, so as a second-year, Monica couldn't be paired with her.

What to do? What to do? As Monica trembled, head still buried in her hands, Isabelle offered a confident proposition.

"If the dorms are what you're worried about, my sister, I have an idea. Allow me to resolve the matter brilliantly and in a way befitting a proper villainess."

"A…a proper villainess…?" repeated Monica, visibly confused.

Isabelle grinned. "You can leave it to me!"

Eventually, the carriage reached Serendia Academy. The building was beautiful, just like the Ridill Royal Palace. White walls and a blue roof—it didn't have the spires the castle did, but it was decorated all over with gorgeous sculptures. Monica looked up at it in a daze.

"Shall we go?" asked Isabelle, prompting her onward.

Instead of heading for the dormitories, though, Isabelle proceeded to the headmaster's office. *If we suddenly request a meeting*, thought Monica, filled with trepidation, *won't the headmaster be cross with us?*

Contrary to her expectations, however, the headmaster was quite obsequious in accepting their request, rubbing his hands together all the while.

Isabelle's family, House Kerbeck, was famous—in fact, it was one of the top five rural noble houses in the kingdom. Given how much they'd donated to the school, it was no surprise that the headmaster was especially deferential toward Isabelle.

"Oh, why, hello and welcome, Lady Isabelle. As always, I am eternally indebted to your father."

The headmaster was middle-aged and wore his gray hair combed down. His large face was now covered with an ingratiating smile as he guided Isabelle and Monica into his office.

As befitted a school for the children of nobles, Serendia Academy's interior was sumptuously decorated. In particular, they'd clearly spared no expense on the headmaster's office; the walls were adorned with expensive-looking paintings and sculptures and the like.

Isabelle took a seat—by herself—on the sofa across from the headmaster, then ordered Monica to stand behind it. "I come here with a request I'd very much like your help with, Headmaster."

"Oh, oh yes. If there is anything at all that worries you, I will do everything in my power to assist."

As the headmaster smoothly leaned forward, Isabelle took out her folding fan and covered her mouth with it. Then she heaved a sigh that sounded truly melancholy. "I have heard Serendia Academy's dormitories are two students to a room... I am a very delicate and sensitive girl, and I simply couldn't stand to sleep in the same room as someone I've never met."

"Oh! If that is all, you needn't worry. I will prepare an individual room that is worthy of the noble daughter of Count Kerbeck. And now that you mention it, that young lady is a relative, isn't she? Shall I prepare a room for her near yours?"

"Well, I *never*! You would put *her* close to *me*?!" said Isabelle, taking the opportunity to raise her voice. The headmaster shuddered in surprise. Monica, who hadn't been clued in on Isabelle's plan, was also shocked and couldn't help but let out a squeal and shudder.

"You must be joking!" Isabelle continued. "I shall *not* be placed in a room anywhere near this girl who smells of mud!"

"Ahhh, I do sincerely apologize for being so insensitive. I will prepare a room for her as far away from yours as—"

"Headmaster! Even a normal room is unsuitable for this girl! I would feel just *terrible* for whoever was forced to live with her."

When Isabelle tilted her fan and began to fake-cry, the headmaster's hand-wringing accelerated considerably. As he rubbed his palms together in a display of obsequiousness, he said soothingly, "I-in that case, what would you have me do...?"

Behind her fan, Isabelle let slip a smile—she was now certain of her victory. Then she glanced up at Monica, who was hanging her head behind the sofa, and said in a mean-spirited voice, "Why, an *attic room* is good enough for the likes of you… Isn't that right?"

Trembling, Monica eked out a nod. Isabelle turned back to the headmaster and assured him, "She agrees, as you can see."

"An attic room…?" repeated the headmaster, sounding averse. He was probably more concerned about the academy's reputation than he was about Monica.

Isabelle turned a sharp glare on him. "Is it unavailable? If so, a stable would suffice."

"No, no. We'll have a bed brought up to the attic room. Yes, yes."

As the headmaster looked away, Isabelle shot Monica a wink. Monica was totally astonished by this skillful villainess-style resolution.

V-villainesses are pretty amazing…

But it wasn't villainesses who were amazing—it was Isabelle.

* * *

Once she had left the headmaster's office, Monica let out a sigh of relief.

The attic room was above the storage room on the top floor of the student dorms, a different floor than all the other students. Such treatment might have reduced a proper young noble lady to tears, but Monica was incredibly grateful for it.

"I, ummm, Lady Isabelle… Th-thank…"

As Monica attempted to murmur out a thank-you, Isabelle's eyes suddenly got misty. Monica, shocked, looked at her in a panic.

"U-um, Lady Isabelle?"

"Ahhh… If only we could have been roommates! We could have arranged secret tea parties in the middle of the night or crawled under the covers together and shared secrets! But…but I can't allow myself to get in the way of your mission! I fully understand that!"

After wiping her eyes with a handkerchief, she threw her arms around a flustered Monica and clung to the back of her neck. "My sister! If you're ever free, please, please come to my room to visit! I'll do my very best to make you feel welcome!"

"O-okay...," said Monica, nodding stiffly. Isabelle suddenly realized what she was doing and straightened herself out.

They could hear voices from around the corner of the hallway. The entrance ceremony wasn't until tomorrow, but a few teachers and students with club activities could be seen around the school. Thus, it wasn't strange for them to run into someone, but the conversation they were hearing was certainly unusual.

"Damn it! Let me go! Lemme go! I did nothing wrong!"

"Shut *up* already! Or I'll freeze your mouth shut next!"

"Settle down, Cyril Ashley."

"Yeah, Cyril. You're being even louder than *he* is."

From around the corner came three male students and one young male teacher.

A student with black hair was screaming and shouting to be let go, while the other three were restraining him, apparently trying to bring him somewhere.

Isabelle whispered to Monica in a low voice so that only she could hear, "That black-haired young man... That would be Lord Aaron O'Brien of House Steil. I've seen him before at social events."

Aaron was a fairly tall boy, and the other three were having a hard time restraining him despite their number.

Isabelle took out her fan and smoothly covered her mouth. "... The brown-haired boy is Elliott Howard of House Dasvy. I'm not familiar with the silver-haired one, but since he wears the student council emblem, he must be from an elite house as well."

I see, thought Monica. As Isabelle had pointed out, the three male students wore small emblems on their lapels.

Isabelle had both a good memory and a sharp eye—the way she'd recalled their names so quickly and spotted their lapel pins was brilliant.

Monica furtively glanced at her in admiration. *Wouldn't she be much better at infiltration than I would?* she wondered.

In the meantime, the clamorous group of four started heading their way, so Isabelle and Monica both quickly moved to the wall to make room.

The brown-haired boy with the droopy eyes, Elliott Howard, looked toward them and casually raised a hand, saying, "Sorry for the noise."

But right then, the black-haired Aaron—the one being restrained by the other three—looked at the two girls with bloodshot eyes and shouted, "Hey! Hey, you two, say something already! I'm being tricked! I don't... I don't remember, I don't remember, I don't know, I can't recall... Ahhhhh...!"

"Quiet already! Shut your mouth!" barked the silver-haired young man, veins popping out of his temples. He then quickly muttered something.

The muttering brought Monica's head back up. It was a magecraft chant.

And a shortened one, too...!

The silver-haired boy weaved his spell in half the time of a normal chant, then snapped his fingers. Aaron's flailing wrists froze together like shackles. The silver-haired boy then produced a small shard of ice in his palm and rammed it into Aaron's mouth, holding it there.

As the ice shard was shoved into his mouth, Aaron's eyes widened, and he voicelessly screamed.

"Hmph. Hopefully this cools your head a bit," spat the silver-haired boy distastefully.

The droopy-eyed Elliott looked at him in exasperation. "Cyril, did you know all the girls call you the Icy Scion?"

"What is that supposed to mean?"

"It's the name of a character in a novel popular in the capital. Apparently, he's *wonderfully* cool and collected. Why don't you try a little harder to meet their expectations, hmm?"

"I fail to understand. I am always calm."

"......"

Elliott simply shrugged at Cyril—the young silver-haired man.

Finally, the teacher addressed them both and said, "Let's get moving."

"Yes, Mr. Thornlee," answered Elliott without argument.

Cyril looked at Isabelle and Monica and offered a brief apology. Then the three of them dragged Aaron away.

When all four were out of sight, Isabelle broke the silence.

"I wonder if something's happened in the student council."

Speaking of the student council, its president was the target of Monica's assignment—the second prince, Felix Arc Ridill. If there had been an incident in the student council, it meant Monica, his bodyguard, would need to learn the details.

Nooo... I've only just transferred, and I have a feeling things are already getting complicated...

Reflecting on their turbulent encounter with the council members, Monica held her stomach and let out a small groan.

* * *

The attic room Monica was given turned out to be much cleaner than she'd expected. The headmaster had probably seen to it. The room contained both a small, simple bed and a desk for studying—more than enough for Monica.

She raised the window to air out the room, then opened up her travel bag. "Nero, you can come out now... Nero?"

She dumped the contents of her travel bag onto the bed, sending Nero rolling out, too.

"Myaaaahhh..." He made a sound halfway between a yawn and a meow. "Hmm? What's this? Did we arrive already?"

"Mm-hmm. Were you sleeping that whole time?"

"Yep. I can sleep whenever and wherever I want. Pretty great, right?" he boasted.

"Sure," said Monica offhandedly as she picked her coffeepot up off the bed.

The desk that came with the room had several small drawers in it. The bottommost could be locked, so that's where she put the pot.

Despite being one of the greatest mages in the kingdom, Monica had precious few possessions she really cared about. This coffeepot, a keepsake from her father, was far more important to her than her golden staff or the ring and robe signifying the noble rank she had received when she became a Sage.

The pot was her only treasure—she couldn't think of any others.

Nero yawned and looked up at her from the bed after she'd locked the drawer. "So how's school life?"

"Um, they say classes will start tomorrow..."

Starting tomorrow, she would be entering Serendia Academy as a second-year student in the advanced program. And she would be doing so as Monica Norton—not Monica Everett, the Silent Witch. Her face clouded over as she recalled her days at Minerva's Mage Training Institution. For someone as shy as she was, the group life-style of a school was nothing but agony. For the latter half of her time at Minerva's, she had holed up in the lab near-constantly.

"...Ugh. Just imagining it is giving me a stomachache..."

The reason Monica had come here was to secretly protect the second prince. But before she could even think about the mission, in order to not stand out, she would have to live life as a student. Which, for Monica, was going to be difficult.

"Eh, don't sweat the small stuff. Just have a good time with it. Doesn't academy life seem fun?"

"...You only say that because you don't know how scary it is..."

"If it seems like someone's going to find out your secret, you can just use magecraft to handle it, right? Piece of cake. You're an incredible mage, so... Like, couldn't you just control or alter the memories of anyone who finds out about you?"

Nero could be carefree because he knew so little about human affairs. Monica shook her head, a gloomy expression on her face. "Actually, any magecraft that interferes with human minds, like manipulating someone or rewriting their memories—that's all forbidden… If I used it on someone without permission, they'd take my mage certification away from me…"

Magecraft that interfered with someone's mind or mental state was permitted only in very special circumstances, such as when extracting confessions from criminals. Researching it was allowed, and Monica had read a book or two on the subject. However, while she could use such spells if she wished, she didn't particularly want to.

"Spells like those are *really* hard to control. Sometimes people develop side effects, like memory problems or falling into a state of confusion… And I've heard that if it goes really poorly, they might never regain consciousness."

"What? That's terrifying."

"Mm-hmm. So you can't use it for just anything."

Suddenly, Monica recalled Aaron O'Brien, one of the male students they'd passed by earlier today. He had been in a state of confusion, saying he didn't know, didn't remember, and so on. That sounded very similar to the symptoms of someone whose mind had been interfered with using magecraft.

…No, it can't be, thought Monica before shaking her head and turning her focus to preparing for the next day.

"Humans sure do have it rough, huh?" said Nero, his whiskers bobbing up and down.

"Yeah. I wish I could be a cat…," muttered Monica with a dry laugh.

Nero narrowed his golden eyes and stared up at her. "Ever heard of survival of the fittest? It's even worse for cats than it is for *dragons*. I can assure you—if you *were* to become a cat, a crow would peck you to death within minutes."

"…Haah."

She had no answer to that.

CHAPTER 4
The Greatest of Trials
(Self-Introductions)

Monica had never made any effort to remember people's faces. Living by herself in her mountain cabin, she had needed to recognize only the barest minimum of acquaintances.

Unfortunately, as a result, she wasn't familiar with the face of the very person she was supposed to guard—the second prince. And if she was going to be a student here while protecting him, she'd have to memorize the names and faces of everyone around him, too. And so, since coming to Serendia Academy, she was finally putting in the effort to remember people again.

Monica had an easy time remembering people when she wanted to. She had a bit of a special ability: She could, to an extent, measure lengths and angles just by looking at them, without the aid of a ruler or other such device. So all she had to do was compute the widths and angles of a person's facial features and simply remember those numbers.

"Monica Norton, this will be your homeroom teacher, Mr. Thornlee."

On the first day of classes, the headmaster took her to the faculty room and introduced her to a male teacher. The teacher looked around forty, and he wore his gray-streaked black hair combed back. His cheeks were thin, he wore round spectacles, and his facial features made him appear high-strung.

Monica committed the man's face, or rather his numbers, to memory—the angle of his jaw and the width of his eyes.

This is the teacher who was with the student council members yesterday...

Mr. Thornlee didn't seem to remember her, though, as he made no particular mention of the previous day's events. "My name is Victor Thornlee," he said. "I teach fundamental magecraft."

"Mr. Thornlee is a graduate of Minerva's. He has a high-mage certification, as well as several accolades from the Mages Guild for the invention of new magical formulas…"

The headmaster went on, boasting about Mr. Thornlee's history and achievements as if they were his own.

Being an alumnus of Minerva's, the greatest mage-fostering institution in the kingdom, *and* having a high-mage's license made him an elite among elites. Monica could understand why the headmaster would be so proud of having the man as a teacher. Knowledge of magecraft was considered a type of refinement for aristocrats, after all.

"Mr. Thornlee has also been adviser to the student council for five years now. It is difficult to understate how much of an honor it is to be the adviser to Serendia Academy's student council—"

"Headmaster, we must be going soon," interrupted Mr. Thornlee, checking the pocket watch in his left hand.

The headmaster grinned and gave a smooth apology before going back to his seat.

Mr. Thornlee fussily adjusted his glasses, then looked at Monica as if evaluating her. "By the way, I still haven't heard you introduce yourself."

"Um… Well…" Monica looked down and began to fidget with her fingers.

The teacher turned a sharp glare on her. "Back straight!"

"Y-yes, sir!"

The reprimand caused her to give a start and stare back up at him. She was still too scared to look him straight in the eye, though. As her gaze drifted, Mr. Thornlee gave an ostentatious sigh. "Serendia Academy is one of the greatest schools in the land. We expect a certain degree of character and an impeccable level of culture in our students' attitudes."

Monica could tell he was implying she lacked both. In truth, she'd been a commoner before her appointment to the Seven Sages, so she really didn't have the "culture" that came with a noble upbringing.

"Can you at least offer me a proper greeting?"

"I'm, I-I'm so...sor—"

"Lamentable," said Mr. Thornlee, cutting her off midway through the awkward apology and walking away. "Class is beginning. Come with me."

"Y-yes, sir..."

"Back straight!" he barked.

Monica, half in tears, fixed her posture and followed him.

Though she usually stuck with her favorite timeworn robe, today she wore the Serendia Academy uniform: a mostly white one-piece dress with a bolero over the top and a pair of white gloves. Even at Minerva's, noble children would choose to wear their own pair of gloves, but here at Serendia Academy, they were part of the uniform. Monica kept clenching and unclenching her hands, not able to get used to their sensation. Inside the gloves, her palms were slick with sweat.

Eventually, they arrived at the classroom, where Mr. Thornlee had her stand in front of the podium.

"Everyone, your attention, please," he announced. "A new student will be joining us today—Lady Monica Norton."

Her classmates' eyes were all focused on her. That alone was enough to make her dizzy. She felt like a criminal standing trial.

"Please introduce yourself," prompted Mr. Thornlee.

Monica's throat began to seize up. Just being exposed to people like this was almost unbearable, and now he wanted her to introduce herself!

I have to...say something... In times like these, Louis had taught her, all she needed to do was say *my name is*, then her name, then bow or curtsy. But for Monica, even that was a daunting trial.

She opened her mouth to try anyway but managed only to flap her lips without actually saying anything.

Mr. Thornlee gave a particularly audible sigh, not bothering to hide his exasperation. It was like a knife in her heart.

"All right," he said, "take your seat. Yours is the farthest one back along the wall next to the hallway."

Still unable to respond, Monica headed for her seat, legs shaking. Eventually the lesson began, and Monica's brain absorbed absolutely none of it.

* * *

"Excuse me?"

Monica had been sitting stock-still in her chair—despite the start of break time—when she heard a voice from right next to her. Was someone speaking to *her*? But what if they had the wrong person? Monica found herself unable to look up or respond.

This time, the person tapped her shoulder. "Look, I'm trying to talk to you here, *new student*."

Monica gave a start, then awkwardly lifted her face.

Looking down at her was a girl with flaxen hair. She was fair-skinned, with large eyes, and gave off a spirited air. Her hair was done up in intricate braids, and equally intricate-looking earrings hung from her ears.

"I'm Lana Colette," said the girl, giving Monica a close inspection from head to toe before putting her hand on her waist. "Hey, why do you wear your hair in basic braids like that? You look like a country bumpkin. Nobody else at this school styles their hair that way."

As Lana pointed out, Monica's light-brown hair was parted into two loose, simple braids. Louis had taught her several hairstyles befitting a noble girl, but they were all too complicated, and she couldn't remember any of them. The noble girls who had brought a servant to the dorms could have their servant style their hair, but of course Monica didn't have anyone like that.

"I—I…I don't really…know any, um, other…way…"

And just like that, everyone staring at Monica seemed to say with their gaze, *That figures.* With that statement, she had disclosed that she hadn't brought a servant with her. Most of the students who hadn't brought one had a reason.

"Where were you raised?" asked Lana.

Monica's breath caught in her throat. She'd been born and raised in a town relatively close to the royal capital, but right now, she had to pretend to be related to House Kerbeck.

"…L-L-Liannack…," she offered. It was the name of one of the towns in the count's territory.

"Oh!" exclaimed Lana, her eyes widening. "The large town by the kingdom's border! They get imports of rare cloth from our neighbor, right? Hey, what kind of styles are in fashion in Liannack right now? What kinds of dresses do they wear? And what kinds of scarves?"

The barrage of questions put Monica at a complete and total loss. She wasn't actually from Liannack to begin with, and even if she *had* lived there, she wouldn't have known a thing about the latest fashions.

"I, um, I don't really…know much about…that stuff… I'm sorry…"

Lana pursed her lips at the mumbled apology and frowned. "Hey, why don't you wear any makeup? You should at least use powder and lipstick, right? Look at my lipstick. It's the newest item from a makeup shop in the capital."

After that, Lana began to nitpick almost every part of Monica's outfit. "Oh, gloves with embroidery on the edges are the cutest," she said. "I can't believe you aren't wearing a single accessory" and "Those boots are way out of fashion."

Monica could only apologize and say, trembling, that she didn't really know one way or the other.

She really *didn't* understand anything Lana was saying. Lana's hairstyle was very intricate, with beautiful hairpins. Her necklace was lovely as well, and the ribbon at her neck was adorned with splendid embroidery. Though she wore the same uniform as Monica, Lana's made a completely different impression.

SERENDIA ACADEMY
SECOND-YEAR
Lana Colette

Seeing Monica in a fix, the female students around them began to put their fans to their lips and whisper to one another.

"Didn't her father *just* become baron? And now she's bragging about it to a country girl."

"Nobody else will talk to her, so country girls are all who're left."

"She must really be desperate, since they *bought* their noble title and all."

Their voices were low but still loud enough for Monica to hear. Obviously, Lana could hear them as well. The latter's dainty eyebrows began to twitch, and eventually she brushed her flaxen hair back and sniffed. "Hmph. I've had quite enough of this. It's boring talking to you anyway."

"...I'm sorry."

Monica was used to being called boring. She was painfully aware of how dull she was. The topics that excited others fell flat with her, and she knew nothing of the latest trends. Her only interests were mathematics and magecraft. Because of that, all she could do was keep her head down, not make eye contact with anyone, and wait it out. She was looking down now, too, stiff as a stone.

Suddenly, Lana reached out and grabbed Monica's braids. Monica gave a terrified yelp, but Lana told her to "just stay still," her tone sharp.

Then Lana undid Monica's braids and started re-braiding them. Since there was no mirror here, Monica couldn't see what was happening on her head.

Eventually, Lana nodded in satisfaction. "That should do," she said. "See how simple that was? Now, learn how to do it for yourself!"

With that, Lana strode boldly back to her seat. Nervously, Monica touched her fingertips to her head—and felt a ribbon hanging there, smooth and soft to the touch.

* * *

Most students at Serendia Academy ate lunch at the school cafeteria. Not only did the cafeteria feature an array of first-rate chefs, it also had a full waitstaff. They performed simple taste tests on every batch of food to check for poison as well, so the students could enjoy their meals in peace.

A select few students had brought their own chefs or waitstaff to the dormitories, and they'd eat in their room after having the food cooked in the cafeteria. The second prince, whom Monica was supposed to be guarding, was apparently one such student.

Which means there's no reason for me to go to the cafeteria...

Using that as an excuse, Monica snuck out of the classroom once lunch break began. All her classmates were streaming toward the cafeteria, but Monica went against the tide and exited the school building.

She had about a handful's worth of berries in her pocket, and she was hoping to find somewhere to eat them without many people around. Monica had always been good at finding isolated places. When she went to Minerva's, she'd always holed up in a secret spot to read books on magecraft and mathematics. Since the weather was nice and there wasn't much wind today, Monica decided to take a walk outside.

Serendia Academy was located on a very large plot of land, and its gardens were beautifully maintained. Summer's flowers had withered, replaced by the buds of autumn roses that had just begun to bloom.

For the most part, schools attended by nobles began the year in autumn, and commoner schools opened their doors in spring. From spring to summer, nobles were busy with events for the social season, and autumn was when commoners harvested their crops. The school year for each group was set up so as to avoid those times of the year.

Though Monica was of common birth, she'd never gone to a school with the other kids in town. Her father had been a very knowledgeable man and had been able to personally teach her while he was alive. After his passing, her father's disciple—through some twists and turns—had become her foster parent and had enrolled her at Minerva's.

That was why Monica wasn't accustomed to communal living. Even when she'd gone to Minerva's, she hadn't had anyone there she could call a friend.

...Well, there was *one* person, but they'd said their final farewells already.

Still, because of her talent at magecraft, Monica had been allowed to hole up in the lab at Minerva's. But here at Serendia Academy, that wasn't possible.

Magecraft-related courses were available as electives here, but revealing her abilities would complicate matters. With her level of social anxiety, unchanted magecraft was the *only* kind she could use. And if anyone here found out that she could cast without chanting, they'd realize she was the Silent Witch.

Sighing to herself, Monica touched the ribbon in her hair. *I didn't... I didn't even say thank you*, she thought. It was always like this. The things she wanted to say would stick in her throat, and she'd end up swallowing them back down without saying anything at all.

If I can't even have a conversation with a classmate, how am I supposed to get close to the prince? She would need to do so in order to guard him, but he was a third-year student, and she was only a second-year. They were in different grades right from the start.

...If the goal was to guard the prince, then Mr. Louis could have made it so I was in the same grade as he is... No, wait, if he was really serious about it, he'd have sent a man. After all, the girls' and boys' dormitories are separate here!

Louis Miller may have been arrogant with a deeply flawed personality, but he *was* talented. He knew very well that this mission couldn't be allowed to fail under any circumstances. And yet, his "plan" to protect the prince was full of holes. Even just sending someone extremely shy like Monica into the academy had been reckless. *I wonder if Mr. Louis has something else in mind...*, she mused.

As she was cutting through the gardens, she suddenly spotted a large fence near the back of the campus. The academy's plot of land stretched beyond it, but everything that way was cordoned off on the other side of a metal gate. A placard was hung on the gate door that read, OLD GARDENS, UNDER MAINTENANCE, but a closer inspection revealed the gate itself wasn't locked.

…I doubt many people go in there.

After making sure no one else was around, Monica hurried into the old gardens. Enclosed spaces like these made perfect hiding spots.

The foliage here wasn't that rough, despite the UNDER MAINTE-NANCE sign she had seen on the gate. However, she barely saw any flowers at all. Apparently, they'd moved them to the beds out front. The only things that were blooming here were the wild autumn grasses.

But it's a nice, quiet place… I should be able to relax here for a while, thought Monica, cheering herself up just a little and searching for a good spot to sit down. However, her light steps stopped dead after she turned past a cluster of azaleas.

Farther back in the gardens, at the edge of a worn-out fountain, a blond-haired young man sat reading. With his head down, she couldn't make out his face, but his uniform was that of an academy student.

Monica's face fell. She had been so sure this would be a good hiding spot, but someone had beaten her to it. *Guess I'll find some-where else*, she thought, shoulders drooping. But as she turned to leave, she heard a rustling through the grass behind her.

By the time she realized something was happening, an arm had grabbed her wrist from behind. She yelped.

"Caught you!" came the sharp voice of whoever was holding her as her breath caught in terror. "You walked right into my trap!"

Monica craned her neck to see over her shoulder and found a brown-haired young man looking down at her. His features were somewhat mature, with droopy eyes. She remembered his face—specifically, the angle at which his eyes drooped. This was one of the student council members who had been making a ruckus yesterday in the hallway.

If I remember what Lady Isabelle said…this would be Lord Elliott Howard of House Dasvy.

Elliott was gripping Monica's wrist with far too much force for this to be some kind of prank. And he wasn't even trying to hide the hostility in his eyes as he looked at her.

Elliott patted Monica's pocket. He frowned; he could tell something was there, even through the fabric. "What's that in your pocket? A weapon?"

"N-no, it's—it's my...my lunch..."

He laughed scornfully at her desperate explanation, as though it was absurd. "There's no student at this academy who would put their lunch in their *pocket*."

"Ahhh..." He was right—no noble girl who went to Serendia Academy would ever bring berries with them for lunch.

When Monica remained silent, Elliott gave an intrepid smirk and gazed down at her. "I know the face of just about every single student here except first-years. Judging by your uniform's scarf color, you're a second-year. But I don't recall ever seeing you. So it would only make sense to assume you're an infiltrator disguised as a student, right?" He paused for effect. "Now confess! Who hired you?"

Monica *had* passed by Elliott yesterday, but it had been for only a very short time, and she'd been looking down. He probably hadn't gotten a good view of her face. Intimidated by the enmity in his voice, she started to tremble like a small animal.

No, no, no, no, no, no, no! I'm scared, he's scary, this is scary!

Having fallen into a panic, she quickly cast a wind spell without chanting. It wasn't harmful in the slightest—the gust was only enough to make someone stagger.

The dirt the wind kicked up, however, happened to hit Elliott right in the eyes. He let go of her and rubbed at his face.

I...I have to use this chance to get away...

Monica, blind with adrenaline, slipped from Elliott's grasp and began to flee...or at least, she *tried* to. She was hopelessly uncoordinated; when she turned around, her foot twisted, and she fell over on the spot.

She gave a silly-sounding yelp as she hit the ground; the impact caused the berries to fly out of her pocket and scatter everywhere.

"Oh no, oh no, oh no…"

As she tried to get up, completely flustered, someone grabbed her arm. Nervously, she turned around and ended up looking straight into Elliott's droopy eyes.

"You're. Not. Going. Anywhere."

"N-noooooo!"

As Monica broke into loud bawling, the blond-haired young man, who had been watching the exchange from his seat on the edge of the fountain, opened his mouth to speak.

"Elliott, let the girl go."

"What? But why? If she came all the way here, she *can't* be an academy student. I'd bet you anything Aaron sent her as an assassin to—"

Before Elliott could finish his sentence, the blond boy raised his index finger to his mouth. The former stopped talking, seeming embarrassed, and released Monica's arm.

As she sat there in a daze, the blond young man squatted down next to her and picked the berries up off the ground. Monica gave him another look; he had very handsome features. Framed by long eyelashes, his eyes were mysterious—a bright sky blue with just a hint of green in them.

"I heard a new second-year student joined us this year. Would that happen to be you? What did they say your name was…? Ah yes. Lady Monica Norton."

Sniffling loudly, Monica nodded.

The blond young man, still gathering the berries, looked at Elliott. "See? She isn't an assassin—just a little squirrel who happened to get lost." He took Monica's hand and placed the berries he'd picked up into her palm. "I'm sorry we got in the way of your lunch."

Monica tried to thank him—he'd gone through the trouble of kneeling to gather the berries. But she was so nervous that she couldn't form words. *I have to properly tell him thank you…*

As her mouth formed a *th* shape, lips trembling, the young man suddenly looked up, then put his arms around her and pulled her close.

"Watch out!"

"…Huh?"

Monica followed his gaze and noticed something hurtling down from overhead. If they did nothing, it would fall on one or the other of them.

Wasting no time, she silently used a spell to create a strong wind. The gust blew into the falling object just enough so that it landed beside them instead of on top of them.

The object made a crashing noise and broke into several pieces—it had been a flowerpot, and it had fallen from right above them. Depending on where it hit, it could have caused more than a simple injury.

"It's a good thing that wind blew through… Are you all right?" asked the young man, still holding Monica and sounding worried.

Monica, however, was in no state to reply. First, she'd been mistaken as a suspicious person and restrained, then a flowerpot had almost fallen on her head, and now she was being held in the arms of someone she'd only just met. Her mind simply couldn't keep up with the string of unexpected events. She'd been stretched to the breaking point—and *snap!*

"…Ugh."

Monica's eyes rolled back in her head. Frantic, the blond young man caught her before she could fall to the ground.

* * *

A large black shadow stood before Monica's eyes. It flickered and swayed as if cast by the light of a candle. As she gazed up at it in a daze, she thought, *Oh no. He's been drinking again.*

The black shadow looked at Monica, ranting and raving. It was best not to say anything unnecessary in situations like this. So she kept her mouth shut, looked down, and thought about "Old Man Sam's Pigs."

One pig, one pig, two pigs, three pigs, five pigs, eight pigs, thirteen pigs, twenty-one pigs…

I was so happy when I realized that, aside from one, no two adjacent numbers have a common factor... When I told Dad that, he praised me for noticing it...

As Monica mused vacantly, the black shadow swung the alcohol bottle in its hand down toward her. There was a loud crash. Shards flew everywhere—shards of the bottle? No. No, it was...

...It was a flowerpot.

"Wah!"

Monica bolted upright, then gripped her chest to try and quell the incessant pounding of her heart. She had the feeling she'd just had a scary dream. The back of her head throbbed dully.

She exhaled. As she was getting her breathing under control, she heard a voice from right next to her hesitantly ask, "Are you all right?"

Monica awkwardly turned her head to look. A female student she didn't recognize was gazing at her with worry. She was a short girl, with hair the color of hazelnuts and a calm demeanor about her.

"Who...a-are you?" stammered Monica awkwardly, shy as ever.

The girl gave a faint smile. "Selma Karsh. We're in the same class—I'm the class health officer. I heard you had collapsed and were brought to the infirmary, so I came to see how you were doing."

Oh, she thought. *I'm on a bed in the infirmary.* The blond young man had probably carried her here.

What was going on with them? she wondered. She'd only been looking for a place to eat her lunch. But instead, for some reason, she'd been mistaken for an intruder and almost hit by a flowerpot... She felt like so much had happened, and just in the span of her lunch break.

It had been pure luck that she'd been able to evade the flowerpot with her spell. If she'd been just a moment later, it would have been too late, even omitting the chant.

As she began to tremble, recalling the fear she'd felt, Selma reached out a pale hand and gently fixed Monica's messy bangs.

Those slender white fingers and light-pink nails—Selma's hands were completely free of scratches or scars. They were the hands of a maiden who had never done any real work. And they were completely different from Monica's, covered in writing callouses.

"Classes are over for the day, so if you want to return to your dorm, go ahead. I'll tell Mr. Thornlee that you woke up."

Saying no more, Selma quietly left the infirmary.

The sky outside the window was dyed the reds of sunset. Quite a lot of time had passed while she'd been sleeping. Monica got out of bed, then plodded back to her dorm, head hanging.

She hadn't been around this many people in a long time, so her body and mind were utterly exhausted. Her feet were so heavy, she felt like they were bound with lead shackles.

At the girls' dormitory, with dinner approaching, the female students were standing in small groups here and there, entertaining themselves with light conversation. Monica kept her gaze firmly down and away from all of them as she made her way up to the top floor. Walking in the corners away from prying eyes was custom for her—whether in this academy or in town. It had been since long ago. She'd always been an outsider, unable to blend in where people congregated.

Eventually, she reached the storage room on the top floor. She climbed the ladder in the back and pushed open the door in the ceiling that led into the attic room. The sun had completely set during her slow walk through campus, and now the room was just dark enough that she couldn't see her own hands in front of her face.

Monica used an unchanted spell to light the candlestick. People praised her unchanted magecraft as a miracle, but for her, having a normal school life was far more difficult.

She removed the ribbon Lana had used to tie her hair and set it on her desk. Then she spread out a handkerchief and placed the berries on top—they had still been in her pocket.

…*Tok-tok*. She heard a knocking at the window.

When she looked over, she could faintly see the outline of a black cat against the night. She unlocked the window, and Nero deftly used his front paw to push it open.

"Welcome back, Nero."

"Yep, I'm back. And with a whole load of information to boot! Compliment me!"

"…Mm-hmm. Thank you."

"Listen and be amazed! The second prince is a third-year student and the student council president."

These were facts she'd known for a while now. But Monica didn't have the heart to say so in the face of Nero's efforts, so she simply listened to him without speaking.

"That means that if you became a student council member, you could naturally stay close to him! I'm a genius!"

Nero's suggestion was right on the mark. Given that the second prince and Monica were a grade apart, it would be tough for her to make contact with him normally. If she was part of the student council, however, the opposite would be true. But…

Monica fell face-first into her bed and wailed, "But I could never do that!"

Stellar grades were a nonnegotiable condition of becoming a student council member. You also needed to have connections to current members.

Nero gazed at her with his golden eyes. "Wait. I thought you were one of the Seven Sages, Monica. Aren't you a genius? You do a bang-up job on your next test, and I'm sure you'll be able to…"

Monica shook her head wordlessly, then lined her textbooks up on her bed. An overwhelming portion of them were on history or languages. Those *were* the fields of knowledge noble children were expected to have, after all.

But Monica's focus had been magecraft and everything about it. She was quite familiar with magecraft history, magecraft fundamentals, magical biology, magical engineering, and law topics related to magecraft, but as for just about anything else, save mathematics, she was below average. Her ability to memorize things was heavily skewed: While she could commit anything that had to do with magecraft to memory, as for other things…well, she couldn't even list the five noble ranks in order.

"You went to that other school, right? Minerva's, yeah? Didn't you learn any language stuff there?"

"…A-at Minerva's, I focused on…ancient magic script and spiritspeak…" Neither of those was a subject usually taught to nobles. Most people went their whole lives without ever touching upon either of them.

Monica held Nero to her chest and hung her head. "What should I do? Oh, what should I do…?" At this point, she was in no position to protect the second prince. It would take everything she had just to avoid failing out of the academy.

Actually, she had an even more fundamental issue…

"A lot of people were very kind to me today," she said, glancing at the ribbon and berries sitting on the desk.

Lana had been overbearing, but she *had* been the first in class to speak to her. And the young man she'd met in the old gardens had picked up her berries for her. Isabelle had already done so much to support her, and Selma, the health officer, had come to check on her.

"To tell the truth, I wanted to properly say *thank you* to them, but I…" Her shoulders drooped again.

Nero looked up at her. "Wait, but can't you say *thank you* to me just fine? You just did. I heard you."

"That's because you're not human, Nero…"

The cat made a difficult expression—a very human one. Then, seeming to have thought of something, he waved his tail and jumped out of Monica's lap. "All right, all right. In that case, why don't I help you? You and me, we'll get you over that shyness of yours."

"Nero? Y-you don't mean…?"

"Indeed I do."

Nero hopped up onto a chair, then gave his tail a swish. Instantly, his form bent and squished until he became a clump of black shadow.

Eventually, that shadow swelled, expanded, and took the shape of a human.

In the space of two blinks, the shadow gained color, taking on the hue of healthy skin, as though ink were being washed from it.

"See? How about this?"

The creature sitting on the chair was no longer a black cat—it was a young man who appeared to be in his midtwenties with black hair and golden eyes. His body was wrapped in an old-fashioned robe.

Of course, he wasn't really a human. Nero had merely taken on the shape of one. Monica knew he was capable of assuming human form, and she'd seen him like this several times already.

Nevertheless, the fact that an adult man was now right in front of her caused Monica's body to cower unconsciously.

She managed a couple of squeaks in protest. Her eyes, blank and turned downward as always, had opened as wide as they could, and her slender body trembled. She made herself as small as she could on the bed and covered her head with her hands as if to protect herself.

"No... I, no, I can't... Nero, please... Go back to...to being a cat..."

Monica was on the verge of tears, and Nero pouted. The act made him look considerably younger. "No. Way. You manage to talk to Lou-lou-lou Lountatta just fine, don't you?"

It appeared Nero had no intention of remembering Louis Miller's name. Monica corrected him and defended herself.

"It's Louis! And if I don't answer him properly, he twists my ear!"

"Whoa... Is that guy for real? What a jerk. Don't worry—I won't twist your ear or anything. How's that, huh? Pretty nice of me, right?"

Actually, Louis was the extreme one here. What Nero was proposing was normal.

Nero hummed with pride, then pressed further. "Now, be grateful, worship me, and say thank you!"

As he inched closer, Monica bent back, and her mouth flapped open and closed. "Eep...! Ah, ah... Th... Tha... Tha-th, th..."

After managing to squeeze out the first three letters, Monica's mouth began to produce garbled, meaningless words mixed with heavy breathing, in and out. Out of context, she would have appeared ill.

Nero turned away like a sulking child. "Hmph. I get it. You're not grateful that I snuck into the school and got all that information for you, huh? I don't know if I can ever recover from this shock. I'm so hurt!"

"I—I didn't— I'm so…"

"I want to hear *thank you*, not *I'm sorry*. Come on. You've got to thank your precious familiar properly, Master," said Nero, legs dangling impolitely as he sat on the chair.

Monica squeezed her eyes shut, clenched her fists in her lap, and mustered up her voice. "Th-thank you, like always, Nero!"

"Hey, there you go! That's the ticket. Next, say, *Nero is the greatest!*"

"Nero is the greatest!"

"Nero is so wonderful!"

"Nero is so wonderful!" repeated Monica, her eyes spinning at this point.

Nero scratched his cheek. "…I'm starting to feel like I'm brainwashing a good person."

"Nero, you're terrible…"

"Meow?! I was doing this for you… Hmm?" Nero's golden eyes swiveled to look through the window before he proceeded to open it and lean his whole body out.

Monica hastily tugged the hem of his clothes. "N-Nero! It's…it's dangerous! You'll fall…!"

"Hey, Monica, look. That guy in the boys' dormitory yard looks suspicious."

"…Huh?"

She got up next to him and leaned out the window herself, then directed her gaze toward the boys' dormitory. She had a good view from her attic room window, but there was no moon tonight, so she couldn't discern anything very far away.

Silently, she used a spell to improve her vision over long distances and in low light. It wouldn't let her see through obstacles, though. That was why she'd had to lean out the window.

...He's right... Someone's in the yard of the boys' dormitory...

The person was wearing a hooded cloak, so she couldn't see their face. But she did get a glimpse of golden hair fluttering inside the hood.

Just then, a gust of wind swept off the figure's hood.

From where she was, Monica could see only the back of the person's head. Immediately, she burned the head's dimensions into her memory.

The person stopped moving and pulled the hood back up, but the wind blew again, giving her a moment's glimpse beneath the cloak. Underneath, they were wearing a fine frock coat. Monica visually measured the length of their torso and legs before the figure crossed through the dormitory yard and disappeared around a corner of the building.

Nero narrowed his eyes, frowning. "Can't see him anymore. Any magecraft useful for this situation?"

"...He went behind the building, so I can't track him any farther... But..."

Monica put a finger to her chin and closed her eyes. Numbers flew through her mind at a dizzying pace.

And those numbers told Monica one fact.

"I've... I've met that person before."

CHAPTER 5
The Silent Witch Speaks Fervently on the Golden Ratio

When Monica was about five, she had begged and begged her father for a certain object. The object she had wanted so badly was a tape measure.

Monica had learned her numbers and basic arithmetic faster than the other children her age; at five, she already knew from her father—a scholar—how to measure area and volume.

And so, she had asked for a tape measure because she'd wanted to find out the area and volume of the things around her.

Her father's friend, who happened to be there at the time, was completely taken aback when he heard her request. But when Monica's father heard her reasoning, he had smiled gently and given her a tape measure as a gift, just as she had asked.

Having acquired the object of her desires, Monica lost herself in measuring all the furniture in the house, as well as the sizes of her own limbs and her father's.

"The world is filled with numbers," Monica's father had often told her. "Humans are the same—our bodies are made up of vast quantities of numbers."

Each time she used her tape measure to figure out the area or volume of a nearby object, she felt in her bones how correct her father had been.

For young Monica, this had been an irrepressible source of joy and happiness.

* * *

...I walked around with that tape measure until the division markings wore down beyond recognition, didn't I?

As her half-awake brain lingered on a dream of her childhood, Monica turned over in bed, at which point the morning sunlight coming in through the window made her face scrunch up. Slowly, she rose. The attic room didn't have any curtains, giving the morning sun free rein.

Once Monica had gotten out of bed, the first thing she did— before even taking care of her appearance—was bring her coffeepot out of the drawer. Then she used an unchanted spell to create water and filled the pot with it.

It was said that water fabricated with magic was unsuitable for drinking, due to the mana it contained.

A human body could retain only so much mana, so consuming a large amount of mana-rich water would lead to magic poisoning. That was why Monica normally drew her water from a well.

But a little bit wouldn't hurt. As one of the Seven Sages, Monica could store a higher amount of mana than normal people anyway. It wasn't easy for her to come down with magic poisoning.

She filled the pot with the water she'd created, ground some coffee beans, and set them up on the pot. Then she took out a small metal trivet, placed the pot on top of it, and used another unchanted spell to create fire. Because a caster needed to maintain the intensity of the heat as well as its position, even a small flame like this required an intricate spell and quite a bit of control.

Nero, who was lying on the bed in his black-cat form, looked at her with mild exasperation. "Using your skills just to make a cup of coffee? Isn't that a bit of a waste?"

"W-well... I can't just use the kitchen without asking, so...," said Monica softly in protest, pouring the coffee from the pot into the cup.

Nero jumped up onto Monica's desk and gazed at her with his golden eyes. "Monica, I want to try some of that."

"Really? Why?"

"I read it in a novel recently. Bartholomew, the protagonist, drinks coffee in silence—it's very cool and refined."

Monica thought for a few moments, then scooped up a little of the coffee from her cup with a spoon and placed it in front of Nero. Coffee probably wasn't the best thing to give a cat, but Nero wasn't a normal cat, so he'd be all right. Probably.

"Are you sure?" she warned. "It's pretty bitter."

"When a creature loses his sense of adventure, he atrophies."

"...Was that in a book, too?"

"You bet. Dustin Gunther is the greatest."

After naming one of the capital's trendiest novelists, Nero gave the coffee in the spoon a quick lick. Immediately, the fur covering his entire body bristled.

"Hogyah-rah-phah!" he cried out—a peculiar exclamation neither human nor feline—and began rolling around atop the desk.

As she had expected, it didn't seem to be to his taste. Nero let out a ragged breath, like a warrior just returned from the brink of death, then looked up at Monica.

"Yes, that certainly excited my sense of adventure. You must have some messed-up taste buds to be able to drink *that* and enjoy it."

"......"

Monica ignored him and sipped her own coffee.

Hot and bitter as it flowed past her tongue, the liquid woke her hazy mind right up.

Suddenly, her father's words came to mind: "First, eliminate the unnecessary. Once you have done that, the remaining numbers will be exceedingly simple."

...But what's unnecessary? she thought. For example, morning coffee certainly wasn't unnecessary for her. It was important. But for those who hated coffee, such a custom may have seemed pointless. *If only it were a formula. Then I could solve it right away.* How difficult it was to suss out the unnecessary in a person's mind.

Still sipping her coffee, Monica glanced at the ribbon and berries on the desk. She'd never cared about her hairstyle before. Prior

MONICA'S FAMILIAR
Nero

to yesterday, she would have said for certain that ribbons were unnecessary.

The berries, too. Monica wasn't overly fond of eating, so if not for the berries, she probably would have shrugged and just gone without lunch. She picked one up and popped it into her mouth. She didn't normally even taste the food she ate, but for some reason, this time, she wanted to eat them with care and attention. So she made sure to pay attention to the flavor before she swallowed them.

"…Hey, Nero… Is there anything you think of as a 'necessity'?"

"Hmm? What's this? Philosophy so early in the morning? …Yes, I know the word *philosophy*. Am I incredibly smart and cool or what?"

"…Yes, you're amazing," said Monica flatly.

Nero pointed his right paw straight at her. "That's it!" he said. "For me, your words of praise are quite the necessity. So give me more! Praise me! Write a ballad for me, in fact! Or a novel! Or paint a portrait—leave something for future generations so they know my greatness!"

That last part was definitely asking too much, but it gave Monica a tiny bit of joy to know her words of praise were needed.

"Also, it's nice to enjoy things that aren't necessary," Nero continued. "'Human life is full of the unnecessary, so why not enjoy it?' That's another quote from one of Dustin Gunther's novels."

For Monica, who had to try her hardest just to live, enjoying the unnecessary seemed like a monumental task. Nevertheless…

"I'll…give it a try," said Monica, picking the ribbon up off the desk. As she did so, she remembered something else her father had told her, his gentle voice replaying in her mind.

It's the most difficult challenges that are the most enjoyable, Monica.

* * *

Lana Colette was sitting at her seat, her chin in her hand, flipping through a textbook.

Once Monica had found her, she managed to walk, legs trembling, to her side.

"I… I'm, um…"

"What do you want?" Lana kept her face toward the page, moving only her eyes to look at Monica—and when they saw her, they opened wide. "What happened to your hair?!"

Monica's hairstyle wasn't what Lana had done for her the day before, nor was it in her usual braids. Instead, the hair on the top of her head fluffed out unnaturally, with two braids forcibly affixed around it. It was rather avant-garde.

"I, well, I wanted to, um, do it like you did…"

"Your basic braids would have been better!"

Monica whimpered as Lana shouted at her. She looked down and shoved her hands into her pockets. Then she pulled out the ribbon she'd borrowed yesterday and nervously held it out to Lana.

"…Here… Um, so…thank…thank you for yesterday…"

Remembering her practice with Nero the night before, Monica squeaked out her thanks. She still sounded like she was about to die, but she'd been able to say the whole thing properly.

However, when Lana looked at the ribbon in Monica's hand, she gave a dismissive sniff and turned away. "I don't need that. It's not in style anymore," she stated brusquely, as if to say the conversation was now over.

Normally, Monica would have withdrawn immediately, tears in her eyes. But instead, she held herself firmly in place and desperately wrung out her next few words. "Would…would you…sh-show me… how to do it…like you did, *p-pleesh*?"

She'd stuttered the last word. She went red up to her ears, and since she was looking down, she couldn't see that the corners of Lana's mouth were twitching as she tried her best to hold in laughter.

"Well, I suppose you've given me no choice! Sit right there, okay?" said Lana haughtily, gesturing with her chin toward a place beside her.

Monica brought her chair over as instructed and sat down.

Lana speedily undid Monica's hair. "Really, how on earth did you manage to come up with something so odd?! It's unbelievable! Hey, do you have a comb?"

"N-no…," responded Monica weakly.

Lana gave her hair a tug. "…I'm surprised you had the guts to ask me to teach you when you haven't even brought a *comb*."

"I-I-I-I'm…sorry!"

Lana sighed in exasperation, then took out her own comb. It was made of silver, with intricate openwork on the grip. Upon closer inspection, small jewels were embedded in it in the images of tiny flowers.

"Not too long ago, goldwork combs with bird motifs were in fashion," she remarked. "But ones like this are much trendier right now. The smaller number and size of the jewels make it very cute. The craftsmen in Anmel are particularly skilled, so if you want the best, you have to get one from Anmel…"

Then, for some reason, Lana trailed off and began combing Monica's hair in silence.

Why did she suddenly stop speaking? wondered Monica, mystified.

Then Lana whispered something so only she could hear. "It's boring, isn't it? What I'm talking about, I mean."

Monica's eyes widened. It sounded like Lana was sulking. Monica turned to look up at her.

Lana's lips were turned in a frown, and she looked hurt. "My family bought their title, after all. I know you're thinking that the things I say are vulgar and not worth listening to."

"U-um…well…" Flailing her arms pointlessly, Monica frantically worked her mouth. "I—I get told I'm boring a lot, too… Well, because I, um, talk about numbers all the time…"

She could talk about *anything* related to mathematical equations and magical formulas. But she'd forget to pay attention to her listener's reactions and keep talking far too long. Louis Miller had scolded her for it more than a few times. The handsome mage would sometimes twist her ear without mercy, smile, and ask, "Have you returned to this world, my fellow Sage?" Remembering it made her start trembling.

Lana gave a short laugh. "You're so weird."

"I—I am…?"

"Yes. Now face forward."

With practiced motions, Lana tied the sides of Monica's hair into braids. Once she had two, she bunched them with the remaining hair and tied them neatly with the ribbon.

"There, finished. It's not so hard."

"W-wow… That was so fast… Then the positions and angles of the braids are the key? No, wait, I should also consider the ratio of the different clumps of hair—"

"It's not about numbers! You learn with your hands. Now, undo it and try it again yourself."

Monica's eyes widened at Lana's words, and she exclaimed, "What?! But it's so pretty… D-do I really have to undo it…?"

When Lana heard the words "but it's so pretty," her mouth twitched—the compliment seemed to have put her in a good mood—and then she cleared her throat, playing the big sister. "You can't learn it if you don't do it yourself. If you mess up and run out of time, I'll redo it, so give it a try."

"Ugh… It's like breaking apart a neat, finished equation and writing over it with random numbers…"

"What kind of analogy is that…?"

Just as Lana smiled, half-exasperated and half-pleased, a commotion arose in the classroom.

It was still too early for the teacher to have arrived. Wondering what was going on, Monica looked toward the source of the noise. There, she found a male student she recognized—the young man with droopy eyes and brown hair.

I-it's him…

Elliott Howard, the member of the student council who had accused Monica of being an intruder in the old gardens the day before. He took a look around the classroom, and when his eyes met hers, he grinned.

Monica gasped in fright and hid herself behind Lana. However, it was already too late. His leather shoes clapping across the floor, Elliott headed straight for her seat. Monica immediately leaped out from behind Lana and hid behind a nearby curtain.

Elliott sneered at her eccentric behavior. "I can't believe you were really an academy student. In fact, I'm still not entirely convinced. Running away as soon as you see someone's face? No proper lady would do that. I see—you really are a timid little squirrel."

Trembling, Monica looked at Elliott from between the curtains. "I-I'm a h-human…"

"If you're a human, then at least come out from there."

"……"

Hesitantly, Monica came out from behind the curtains, and Elliott smiled. At least, his mouth was shaped like a smile—his droopy eyes were cold.

"I came here because I need something from you," he said. "Would you come with me quietly?"

"I—I have, um, classes…"

"This class's homeroom teacher is Mr. Thornlee, right? I'll have a word with him about it. And it's only the second day of the new semester anyway. They won't cover anything that important." Elliott walked several paces away, then craned his neck to look back at her. "I'm a member of the student council. If you want to get along at this academy, you should do as I say, newcomer."

If Monica cried *no*, burst into tears, and ran away, she'd be no different than she was yesterday. So instead, she took a deep breath, then gave a little nod. "A-all right."

Elliott Howard wasn't even trying to hide his disdain for her, and his words were laced with thorns. Still, it was probably better than a certain Sage she knew, who would send offensive magic flying at her, smiling all the while. At any rate, that was what she told herself as she pushed her shaking legs to start moving.

* * *

Elliott stopped in front of a grand door on the fourth floor. All of Serendia Academy was extravagant enough to rival the estates of high-ranking nobles, but this door was especially splendid.

Elliott gave a light knock, then opened the door without waiting for an answer.

"Coming in."

"Welcome," came a mild voice from inside—a voice Monica had heard before.

Elliott held the door open and urged Monica inside with his eyes. Gripping her fists tightly in front of her chest, she proceeded.

"E-excuse me."

The interior was spacious, with a scarlet rug laid on the floor. Every single room in this academy had extravagant workmanship that was incomparable to any normal school, but this one was particularly lavish. The detailing on the tables, chairs, and pillars was incredibly intricate. The headmaster's room had been sumptuously decorated with rows of paintings and sculptures, but this place evoked a different sort of elegance.

Near the back of the room, a male student sat at an official-looking desk. His hair was honey-blond and shone in the light from the window, and his eyes were beautiful—light blue with just a touch of green.

"I apologize for calling you here so suddenly, Lady Monica Norton," he said.

"Y-you're, um, from yesterday..." This was the young man who had picked up Monica's berries and protected her from the flowerpot in the old gardens. And he wore the same gentle smile now as he had then.

"Were you able to eat your lunch after that, little squirrel?"

"Um, thank...er, thank y-you for yesterday!"

I said it! I managed to say it properly. Monica's goal for today had been to thank Lana and this young man for the day before. She quietly savored her joy at having accomplished both so quickly.

The young man softly tilted his head to the side. "I'm sorry? Did I do something that warranted thanks?"

"Um, you picked up my berries, and…and you brought me to the infirmary…," said Monica, kneading her hands.

The young man's face lit up in understanding. "You don't have to thank me for that. It's the student council president's duty to safeguard the students."

What a kind person, thought Monica in admiration—before processing what he had just said. If she wasn't mistaken, he'd said something rather important. Very slowly, she looked back up and repeated, "Student council…president?"

"That's right." The young man nodded with a smile. He quietly rose and offered Monica an elegant bow. "I suppose I haven't introduced myself yet. I am Felix Arc Ridill, the seventy-fifth student council president of Serendia Academy. It's a pleasure to make your acquaintance, Lady Monica Norton."

"……"

So it turned out that the kind male student from the day before had actually been the student council president. That made him the second prince—and the one Monica was supposed to be guarding. Once she'd understood everything, her first thought was…

"U-um…," she stammered.

"What is it?"

"…If you're a prince, how come you, um, snuck out of the dorm last night?"

Elliott, who had been waiting at the door, flinched and looked toward Felix. "Wait, you snuck out last night? This is the first I'm hearing about it."

Felix deftly avoided Elliott's pointed stare and smiled at Monica. "I'm not exactly sure what you're talking about."

"Um, well, I saw you from my window last night. You were standing outside the boys' dorm…" There was no doubt that the suspicious person Nero had discovered the previous night had been Felix. But why would he be wandering around outside after curfew?

Felix responded to Monica's unassuming question smoothly, his smile never lapsing.

"There was a new moon last night, wasn't there?" He was implying that it would have been too dark to see anything from her window.

When Monica tried to respond, Felix, back at the desk, laced his fingers and rested his chin on his hands. "So you saw someone exit the boys' dormitory in the middle of the night?" he continued. "Can you tell me what they looked like? We'll have to strengthen the academy's security."

"Th-they were wearing a hood, so I couldn't see their face. I only got a brief glimpse of, um, their blond hair and the back of their head…sir."

"Well, we have plenty of blond students at the academy."

The moment she heard this counterargument, a fire lit inside her. It was, perhaps, that particular drive of a scholar to prove her claim. Addressing a perfectly relaxed Felix, Monica clenched her fists and declared, "Th-the hooded person yesterday had the same, um, physique as you."

"It wouldn't be strange for someone to have a similar physique to me, would it?"

"It wasn't just similar—it was the golden ratio!"

"…I'm sorry?"

Once her heart had been set ablaze, Monica ceased to take in her surroundings and became lost in the details of her proof—a bad habit of hers. Fortunately, there just so happened to be a movable blackboard for conferences pushed against the wall. Monica drew a simple picture of a person in it, then drew a rectangle around the head area.

"I am confident in my ability to accurately estimate the length of anything I see. The ratio between the width and height of your head is 1 to 1.618. This number is extremely close to the golden ratio, which humans feel to be the most beautiful. To be precise, the golden ratio is 1 to 1.61803398…and it goes on, but I'll omit the rest."

Without sparing a glance toward her baffled audience, Monica drew a horizontal line through the picture's navel, essentially dividing it into an upper and lower half. Above the line she wrote a 1, and below it she wrote 1.618.

"Even if someone is wearing clothes, you can use the length of their legs to calculate the rough position of their navel. Both you, sir, and the person from last night produce the same golden ratio when your upper and lower body are divided this way. But wait! If we were to use 1 for the lower portion instead, then that would bring your total height, combining the upper and lower portions, to 1.618. The golden ratio again—almost as if it were purposely calculated! This property is extremely rare! If you were to measure yourself with a tape measure, you would see that my theory is...correct..."

It was then that Monica finally emerged from her passionate appeal. Her breathing was still erratic, but the trance was broken.

I... What was I just...? Still gripping the chalk, she awkwardly looked back at Felix and Elliott.

Elliott was standing still, eyes wide.

Felix, on the other hand, was leisurely calculating something, muttering to himself. "Last time I had my measurements taken, the number was..." After a few moments, his face lit up. "Wow, it really is 1 to 1.6."

"......"

"I've been complimented on my appearance before, but never like this," he said, less sarcastically and more as if he found the whole thing very amusing.

Monica unconsciously put her head in her hands. *Ahhhhh! I've done it again...*

She often lost track of what was going on around her when dealing with equations and magical formulas. And every time she did, Louis would end up twisting her ear, but... *I can't believe I did that in front of the person I'm supposed to be protecting, of all people!*

In any case, she needed to stay in Felix's good graces. Desperately, she tried to think of some excuse. Louis had once called her awful at this particular task—so she thought, and she thought, and she overthought. And what she came up with was this:

"The golden spiral, which is based on the golden ratio, uses the sequence of numbers in the song 'Old Man Sam's Pigs' for each radius! In the sequence, the ratio between every pair of numbers gets closer and closer to the golden ratio. It's a beautiful sequence... In other words, 'Old Man Sam's Pigs' is amazing... No, wait, I meant to say, your proportions are amazing! Sir!"

If Louis had been here, he would have asked her what exactly her excuse was supposed to accomplish, then resorted to violence.

Hearing Monica praise both a member of the royalty and a song about pigs in the same breath, Elliott narrowed his eyes and groaned. "What on earth is 'Old Man Sam's Pigs'?"

Elliott didn't seem to recognize the popular children's song, but Felix struck his palm with a fist in recognition. "Oh, the nursery rhyme... I get it. So that's what those numbers are."

Felix seemed honestly impressed, and Elliott narrowed his droopy eyes to stare at him.

"Then the little squirrel *has* proven that you were loitering outside the dorm at night for an undercover investigation."

"Yes, though it didn't bear fruit, unfortunately."

"Cyril would faint if he heard."

"I know. So I was hoping you could keep it a secret."

Judging by their exchange, Felix had been acting as a decoy in order to smoke out some sort of criminal—and without telling anyone about it, at that.

A-as his bodyguard, I can't ignore that..., she thought. But would Felix explain if an outsider like her was to ask him? While Monica was worrying, Felix and Elliott continued their discussion.

"Come on, Elliott, she's clearly a harmless little squirrel. Not only did she take no action after witnessing me last night, but she then accidentally let it slip here. She can't possibly be an assassin."

"But couldn't it all be a ploy to make us drop our guard? The flowerpot incident yesterday was too unnatural. It's entirely possible that Lady Norton here led you to where the flowerpot would fall."

Monica let out a surprised yelp. She sensed even more suspicion being cast her way, and she couldn't merely stand by and let it continue. "U–um, so that flowerpot yesterday…didn't just fall by chance?" she asked nervously.

Elliott glanced at Felix, waiting for his decision.

Felix gave a smile and recrossed his legs in his chair.

"Why don't I explain things from the beginning? It all happened two days ago when we discovered the student council accountant, Aaron O'Brien, had been embezzling funds from the council budget. When we pressed him on it, he fell into a state of confusion… So we decided to confine him to his dorm room until his expulsion was finalized."

Aaron O'Brien was a name Monica remembered. That was the black-haired male student who had been shouting in the hallway two days ago as the others restrained him. Isabelle had told her his name.

"The student council would prefer not to let a source of internal embarrassment become public. We had hoped to keep Accountant O'Brien's embezzlement a secret from the other students, tell them he had suddenly fallen ill and needed to leave school, and wrap things up quietly. Unfortunately, a bit of an incident happened shortly thereafter."

* * *

It was the day before the opening ceremony. Felix had passed judgment on Aaron O'Brien only that morning, and he was working with the other council members to clean up the mess Aaron had left.

The most troublesome aspect was having to review the accounting records. Aaron had altered several items in the process of embezzling funds. Then, to conceal those alterations, he'd fiddled with other numbers—and he'd repeated this process several times. As a result, the ledgers were in a pretty terrible state.

The student council members were all working together to review them, but it would take considerable time to fix all the numbers. That day, they didn't end up progressing very far. Time, however, continued to tick on, and with the opening ceremony coming up the next day, they couldn't afford to devote all their time to revising the ledgers.

Around three in the afternoon, the student council adviser, Mr. Thornlee, made an appearance and said, "We need to prepare for tomorrow's opening and entrance ceremonies."

Felix would have to take charge of setting up for the ceremonies and had to go. He'd need the other male students to help him move things around, too. So he left the record reviews to one of the secretaries, Bridget, and the officer of general affairs, Neil, and took the other two, Vice President Cyril and Elliott, the other secretary, with him to the hall where the ceremony would be held.

The chairs for the new students had already been placed in rows, and a hanging sign was set up near the entrance. With the decorations mostly complete, Felix and the others would just be doing the final checks. Still, as they were running down their list, they noticed small things here and there, such as chairs missing, which needed to be dealt with.

"Let's put the new-student ribbons into boxes according to their class. That'll make the day go more smoothly than if—"

As Felix was giving Elliott instructions, Mr. Thornlee looked above Felix's head and suddenly paled. "Look out!" he cried.

A moment later, Cyril called out, "Sir!" his voice almost a scream.

Hearing Mr. Thornlee and Cyril, Felix moved before his mind could even process what was happening.

A few seconds later, something crashed down where he'd been standing—the sign that had been hanging over the entrance.

This sign had been affixed to an anti-fall grating on the second-story window of the ceremony venue using metal clasps. In other words, someone had reached through the window and unclasped them.

They looked up and saw that the second-story window was slightly ajar—and in the window, they caught sight of a figure, just for a moment, before it quickly withdrew.

* * *

"…And that's the long and short of it."

After listening to Felix's explanation, Monica was ready to faint. He had called it a "bit of an incident," but to any normal person, it was quite literally an attempted assassination.

I—I can't believe an incident like that happened on the very day I arrived here…! Feeling the blood draining from her face and her lips trembling, she looked at Felix and Elliott.

Felix had maintained his serene smile throughout the explanation, but Elliott was scowling. The latter reaction was the proper one in this case. Something was wrong with Felix. How could he smile so calmly when his life was the one being targeted?

O-or maybe members of the royal family are used to that kind of thing, Monica thought in a corner of her mind.

"U-um, did you find out who dropped it…?"

"Unfortunately, they got away from us. Isn't that right, Elliott?"

"…Sorry about that. I wasn't able to catch them," said Elliott with a sulk before offering a few more details.

When the sign had fallen, three people had been with Felix: Mr. Thornlee, Cyril, and Elliott. Mr. Thornlee, being the only teacher present, had entrusted Felix's protection to Cyril and gone with Elliott to chase down the culprit. Unfortunately, they hadn't been able to find anything—even after splitting up to cover more ground.

Felix gave a relaxed sigh and shrugged a little. "It happened a few hours after we found Aaron O'Brien guilty. It's natural to assume the two events are related, isn't it? But when the sign fell, O'Brien was confined to the boys' dorm. That means someone else must have dropped it." He narrowed his blue eyes slightly, then gave Monica a meaningful look. "O'Brien implied he'd had an accomplice in the embezzlement. It's highly likely that person was the one who dropped the sign."

Felix had interrogated Aaron, but by then, Aaron had lost it and could only mutter, "It's their fault… Their fault…," over and over again. He didn't seem to be in a state to talk about his collaborator.

As Elliott explained this, his lips twisted into a sardonic grin. "So we laid a trap to smoke out the collaborator—during lunch break yesterday."

"...Oh, so that's why you were in the old gardens...?"

"That's right."

If Felix was alone in the empty back gardens, the culprit would be highly likely to make another attempt. Their plan had been for Elliott to hide—they would wait for the villain to go after Felix, and then Elliott would restrain them. Unfortunately, Monica had arrived completely by chance.

"I'll be honest. I believe you're working with the culprit, and you intentionally led the prince to where the flowerpot would fall."

Despite having come to this academy to *protect* the second prince, Monica was now being treated like an assassin. If Louis Miller was to hear about this, he'd probably laugh; say, *Ah, everything you do is so unexpected, ha-ha-ha*; and then clench his well-calloused fists.

I—I can't get expelled right after infiltrating! If Louis found out, he'd be furious with me... And if I fail the mission, we might be executed...

Monica shook her head so hard, it almost twisted off. "I—I didn't...do it..."

"Then where were you, and what were you doing, at around three PM two days ago, when the incident occurred at the ceremony venue?"

Twiddling her fingers, Monica traced back through her memories. Three PM two days ago. She'd been cleaning her room and telling Nero she wished she could be a cat.

"Th-that day, I was in the girls' dorm...cleaning my room..."

"Is there anyone who can vouch for you?"

"...No."

The only one with her at the time had been Nero, and she couldn't exactly bring a talking cat in as a witness.

As she looked down, Elliott glared at her as though looking at a convicted criminal. His gaze was like a fist tightening around her heart, and her breathing became short and shallow. She was so nervous that oxygen wasn't getting into her lungs. An awful sweat steadily crept through her gloves.

Once the tension in the air became thick enough to cut with a knife, Felix interrupted and admonished Elliott. "I don't approve of you bullying small animals."

"But you *have* to admit that this little squirrel is suspicious," said Elliott, voice full of thorns. But then he appeared to think of something, and his lips turned up into a mean-looking smile. "I know. Let's do it this way, then. Little squirrel, *you* find the culprit who dropped the signboard and the flowerpot. Then I'll believe that you're innocent."

Monica's eyes went wide at Elliott's proposal. "Um, you want... *me* to do that?"

"The two of us would stand out too much. To be blunt, we don't want to make this into too big of a deal. Even the other council members don't know about our undercover investigations."

"Huh?!" exclaimed Monica, eyes even wider now, as she turned to Felix.

Felix smiled wryly and nodded. "Indeed. In particular, our vice president, Cyril, is something of a worrywart."

That made sense. When Nero and Monica had witnessed Felix the night before, he had been trying to lure out the would-be assassin—and without even telling Elliott about it.

But Felix hadn't been targeted that night, either because the villain was too cautious to take the bait or for some other unknown reason.

If they couldn't find the culprit soon, the case might remain unsolved. Felix and the others would want to avoid that as well.

"So? Will you do it? Will you search for the culprit?" asked Elliott, his mean-spirited smirk all but saying, *You'll fail anyway.*

Monica balled her hands into fists in front of her chest. She didn't like this at all. If it was up to her, she'd have holed up in her dorm room and stayed there. Nevertheless, she was in charge of guarding Felix.

"I'll—I'll—I'll doot…," she answered pitifully.

Elliott grinned evilly and turned to Felix, saying, "You heard her."

Felix looked at Monica with a quiet, impenetrable smile.

"Oh? In that case, it's a pleasure to be working with you, Lady Monica Norton."

CHAPTER 6
Rolling Witch

Once she had agreed to search for the culprit behind both the falling sign and the falling flowerpot incidents, Monica headed straight for the rear gardens. The signboard used in the first crime had been taken away when the enrollment ceremony ended, so there were probably no more clues to be found there.

On the other hand, the shards of the flowerpot hadn't been cleaned up—they were apparently still in the gardens, exactly where they had fallen. Nobody went back there, so there was no possibility of an unrelated third party coming in and disturbing the scene.

When Monica passed through the gate leading into the old gardens, the brush next to her rustled and swayed.

"Hey, Monica. How's guarding the prince going?" Nero jumped out of the bush, then shook the leaves from his fur.

Monica squatted down and met his gaze. "Nero, what should I do?"

"Right. About what?"

"The person who protected me from the flowerpot yesterday ended up being the prince..." This unfortunate turn of events was all down to the fact that she hadn't known what the person she was supposed to guard actually looked like.

Nero swung his tail, then looked up at Monica, eyes serious. "You're *his* guard, right?"

"...Mm-hmm."

"Correct me if I'm wrong, but he's not supposed to be the one guarding you, is he?"

Nero was absolutely right. Monica began to flail her hands about pointlessly as she desperately defended herself. "B-but I made sure to protect him with my unchanted magecraft!"

"Yeah, yeah. So why'd you come here, then?"

"They think I'm working with the person who dropped the flowerpot... And they told me to find the real culprit if I wanted to prove my innocence..."

Nero stayed silent for a few long seconds, then looked up at Monica with a very humanlike expression of exasperation. "You're his *guard*, right?"

"...Yes."

"Correct me if I'm wrong, but it's not a good sign if you're being treated like his assassin, is it?"

Monica didn't even have an answer to that.

"...Oh, I'm just a Sage who got in from the waiting list... I'm incompetent. A shut-in... I want to go back to my cabin already," she whimpered.

Nero heaved a sigh. "You're really a handful, Master. Hey, cheer up. Do you want me to squeeze you with my paws?"

"...Yes."

Monica sniffled and pulled Nero to her face. The cat held up his front paws and used the pads to squish her cheeks. The soft sensation allowed her to regain a little calmness.

Nero waited for Monica to stop crying, then asked, "So you're finding the culprit. What do we do first?"

"Mm-hmm. First, I want to figure out where the flowerpot fell from."

The pot hadn't been cleaned up after the previous day's incident; its shards lay scattered across the ground in the same position as before. Monica picked up a few of them.

"...It looks like it was a large flowerpot for group planting. It was round, approximately this big..." When she said "this big," she used her arms to form a ring.

Nero's ears twitched as he looked at Monica dubiously. "How can you tell what shape it was from just the fragments?"

She looked at him, confused. "That's all you need, though, isn't it?"

"No!"

"Huh," she murmured, tilting her head as she transferred the shards in her hand to her other palm. With just what she was able to stack on one hand, she could make a good guess as to the flowerpot's weight. By looking at the scattered shards, she had calculated the pot's approximate size, shape, and weight.

No dirt on the pot's shards. It was empty—either unused or cleaned in advance...

Envisioning the flowerpot before it had broken, Monica slowly lifted her head to look at the school building. Serendia Academy had many flower-adorned balconies, so most of them were lined with flowerpots. In fact, ones without them were fairly rare. It made sense that Felix had wanted her to investigate.

There was little to no wind yesterday. And taking into account the resistance from the wind spell I used... Monica gauged the school building's height with her eyes, then calculated the flowerpot's rate of descent. The balcony's handrails were somewhat high, so it would have been difficult for someone to throw it down with force. It seemed fair to assume that they had leaned over the railing, then simply let go.

The pot landed on soil, which would have cushioned it somewhat. But the resulting shards are this small, and they're spread out over a large area...

There would be a margin of error, but her look at the flowerpot's remains had given her a general idea of which balcony it had been dropped from.

Right there. Fourth floor, the second balcony from the right.

As she was confirming the room's location, Nero used his front paw to tug at the hem of Monica's skirt. "Monica, I want to go inside the school, too."

"…You can't. If you're discovered, they'll throw you out."

"Like they'd ever do that. Even if they *did* find me, I'm too charming for silly humans to resist."

Maybe the academy's cat lovers would fawn over him, but if someone strict like Mr. Thornlee found him, he'd *definitely* throw Nero out.

"You can't, okay?" repeated Monica before setting off toward the school building to investigate the balcony.

* * *

"Oh, what are you doing here?"

As Monica was climbing the stairs inside the building, she heard a familiar voice from below her. She stopped and turned around. Lana, the classmate who had done her hair in braids earlier, was starting up the stairs, her own flaxen hair swaying.

Wh-what should I do? What do I tell her…? I should keep it a secret that I was asked to investigate the balcony, right? If I just tell her I'm running an errand—would that be all right, I wonder?

Monica stopped where she was, then looked down and started twiddling her fingers. Without a clever excuse, all she could do was mutter *um*s and *ah*s.

Lana looked at her, twirling a lock of hair around her finger. "After you were called to the student council room, you never came back. I was worried."

"…Huh?"

A classmate had been worried about her. That was all it took to make Monica's heart do a little leap. Before she realized it, her expression had softened. Covering her cheeks with her hands, she said awkwardly, "Um, well… They asked me to, um, run a little errand…"

As Monica's gaze swam around the hallway, Lana looked at her, confused. It was probably strange that a student council member would ask a new student like her for a favor.

"Oh. Where are you going?" Lana asked.

"Um... T-to the fourth floor. The second classroom from the end..."

"Oh, that would be music room two. You'll want to come this way, then."

Lana started back down the stairs, beckoning for Monica to follow. Why was she going down? Didn't they need to climb the stairs to get to the fourth floor? Monica thought it was strange but followed the other girl, who gave a sniff of pride.

"At this time of day, this hallway gets crowded because classes are all switching rooms. It's faster to go this way."

Had she surmised how bad Monica was with crowds, or was this a coincidence? Either way, Monica was extremely grateful for the proposal. "Th... Thank *phew*..."

She'd psyched herself up to thank Lana, only to trip over her words as always. Her face went bright red.

Lana couldn't help but start laughing. "You're so weird!" She giggled, clearly entertained—somewhat teasing but still familiar. There wasn't any nastiness in her smile. "You're welcome!" she replied, walking off again with a lightness in her step. "If you need to use the stairs at this time of day, you're better off using the ones to the east. The powder room on this side also tends to be much less crowded."

"...The powder room?"

It didn't make much sense to Monica, but apparently Serendia Academy had *several* rooms for the female students to go and fix their makeup. It struck her yet again that this was a school for the children of nobles.

I can't imagine ever using a room like that..., she thought as Lana suddenly stopped in front of her. The other girl's gaze was on the east staircase. Though they'd supposedly been about to climb those very stairs to get to the music room, Lana was looking up at the landing and scowling, her face sour. On the landing were a few female students having a conversation. One of them seemed to be surrounded by the others.

…Oh, that person… She's…

The one in the middle, eyes troubled and downcast, was the girl with hazelnut-colored hair—Selma Karsh. She was the class health officer who had come to check on Monica after she'd been brought to the infirmary. Around the petite Selma were three other female students. The apparent leader—a girl with caramel hair—had a voice that carried above the others.

"Hey, did you hear the rumors? They're saying Aaron came down with a sudden illness and has to leave school. I heard he used to visit all sorts of nasty shops. I'll bet he got some horrible disease from one of them, don't you think? That's just *awful*, Selma! And after everything you've done for him!"

The other two girls put their fans up to hide their mouths and repeated, "Oh, I feel so bad" and "Yes, how terrible for you." But though they *said* those things, their lips were turned up in disdainful grins behind the fans.

Lana, looking at the caramel-haired leader, murmured sourly, "That would be Caroline." Apparently, Lana knew the girl—but it was clear from her expression that their relationship was not a friendly one.

"Hey, Selma. My family is hosting a ball soon. I'll be sure to invite you!"

"Oh my! That's a wonderful idea, Lady Caroline! The scars of lost love can only be soothed by a new one, after all!"

"And your engagement to Aaron has fallen through anyway, right? You should look for someone else, Selma—someone good!"

At that suggestion from one of her followers, Caroline waved her folding fan and laughed as she gazed at Selma's face.

"Then why not my uncle, perhaps?" she said. "He's looking for a new wife. He's more than thirty years older than you, but he's handsome *and* rich."

Selma wasn't saying anything at this point. She simply clenched her gloved fists, stayed silent, and looked down.

Lana turned back to Monica and whispered in her ear, "Best to walk right past them and not get involved. Let's go, okay?"

Lana took the lead, swiftly moving up the stairs, and Monica hurried after her. Once Lana got to the landing, she said to Caroline, who was blocking the stairs, "Would you mind letting us pass?"

"Oh? Well, if it isn't Lana Colette, daughter of the new baron. Awful manners, as usual. My family is much higher in rank and has a much richer history than yours, you know. I'd think someone like you would at least greet me properly."

At Caroline's provocation, Lana's slender eyebrows shot up. "I had no idea blocking the stairs to have a lengthy conversation was proper manners for a high-ranking family. Anyway, would you mind getting lost already? Ugh, even a fleeing cow moves when its master tugs on the reins... Oh, but I apologize. Your butt is probably so heavy, you don't *want* to move."

"Who did you just call a cow?!" Caroline, now furious, raised a hand and pushed on Lana's shoulder. Lana gave a small yelp and teetered. But since she was already near the landing, she got through with just that—a teeter.

She did, however, bump Monica behind her, knocking her off-balance. The next thing Monica knew, her body had tilted, and she was falling through the air.

"Monica!" Lana turned and held out a hand, but she couldn't reach.

I'm...falling...

At that moment, Monica's thoughts started racing at an amazing speed.

If I use wind magecraft inside, they'll discover I'm a mage. Should I use a defensive barrier around myself? No, I can't. The fall would look too unnatural... Then... Then I...

She immediately put up an invisible defensive barrier without using a chant—but not on her own body. Instead, she used it to fill in the spaces created by the steps.

By using it to make the stairs into a simple slanted plane, she wouldn't suffer much damage even if she hit the ground. She'd used every bit of her precise mana control, said to be the greatest in the kingdom, to extend the barrier over the staircase, and it was onto that barrier that she fell.

As she'd calculated, because she was falling on a flat plane, it didn't hurt that much. It didn't hurt, but...

Stairs had different levels—but her slanted path had none. Which, then, would result in greater momentum?

...It went without saying that the answer was the latter. And as was to be expected, Monica ended up rolling, quickly and with great force.

"Hee-yaaaahhhhhhhhh!"

It was a miracle she didn't bite her tongue at the speed she tumbled down the stairs. The momentum carried her past the stairs and across the floor until she collided with a passing male student.

Monica gave a muffled yelp, which overlapped with a low groan—the voice of whoever it was she'd crashed into. Eyes welling with tears, she got up and apologized profusely to the male student, who was now seated on his rear. "I'm... I'm sorry, I'm sorry, I'm sorry, I'm sorry!"

The person she'd struck was a young man with silver hair tied behind his head. Monica had seen him once before, but her mind was too panicked to process such things at the moment.

"...Are you hurt?" he asked, holding out a hand to try and help her up.

Monica, not even noticing the hand, continued rattling off her apologies. "I'm sorry! I'm sorry for bothering you!"

"......"

The male student wordlessly looked down at Monica. Eventually, his fingers reached for her head. Out of reflex, she put her hands over her head in defense—she thought he was going to hit her. But instead, all his fingers did was gently part her bangs.

"Your forehead is a little red. Did you hit it? Does it hurt anywhere else?"

Monica squeaked out a few incomprehensible sounds, then finally realized the young man wasn't trying to attack her. Far from it—he was worried about her. She felt his fingertips on her forehead; they were just a little chilly.

...? Ice magecraft? But he hasn't chanted... Wait, then is his mana leaking out unconsciously?

As Monica was considering this idea, Lana rushed down the staircase toward her. Monica was glad she'd undone the barrier on the stairs so quickly. Otherwise, Lana would have slid down and fallen right after her. She breathed a sigh of relief.

"Hey! A-are you okay?!" exclaimed Lana.

"...Ah, I... Yes..." Monica nodded.

Lana heaved a deep sigh of relief. She'd been worried about Monica's safety, too. As Monica wondered whether she was supposed to say *thank you for being considerate* or *I'm sorry for worrying you*, the silver-haired boy interrupted.

"What's going on here anyway?" he asked, frowning.

Monica finally remembered who the boy was. He'd used an ice spell to silence Aaron O'Brien back when he'd been causing a scene.

"That's the vice president of the student council, Lord Cyril Ashley," whispered Lana into her ear. That made sense—this young man must have been the "worrywart vice president" Felix had mentioned.

"Can anyone here explain what's going on?" asked Cyril.

Caroline, who was still on the staircase landing, descended the stairs with a relaxed gait, her expression an easy, confident smile. "Lady Lana Colette here was goofing off and pushed a fellow student off the stairs."

"What?!" shouted Lana, aghast. Not only did Caroline show no sign of guilt, she was trying to foist the blame onto someone else. "You were the one who pushed me! Right into Monica!"

"Oh?! Are you trying to shift the responsibility onto me? That's some nerve for a child of the nouveau riche."

The two girls with Caroline voiced their agreement. Reassured, Caroline raised the corners of her lips and cast her upturned gaze at Cyril. "Naturally, Lord Ashley, you would believe me—a member of the historic and respected House Norn—over this newcomer girl, right?"

Lana ground her teeth at Caroline's words.

Monica knew that even if neither she nor Lana was in the wrong, if someone with a higher position said they were at fault, it would be taken as the truth.

"…E-excuse me…!" said Monica nervously.

Cyril's eyes swiveled over to Monica, his arms now folded. Perhaps it was just her imagination, but the air around them seemed to have chilled. His gaze caused her to cower and look down.

This young man had been worried about Monica after she'd fallen down the stairs. But if she was to accuse Caroline of wrongdoing, he probably wouldn't listen. He was a member of the student council—they were in charge of keeping order at the academy. This school reflected noble society, and that meant social status was everything.

There isn't anything I could say to change this… Monica looked with resignation at Cyril, who stood in front of her. She bit her lip.

But still…

If Caroline had claimed not to know what had happened, if she'd only played the innocent, Monica would have given up and accepted it. But she'd laid the blame on Lana instead. If she did nothing, Lana would be treated as the instigator.

She would be accused of a crime she didn't commit.

That's something…I just can't let happen… Monica opened her mouth; the blood had drained from her lips. *Please don't give out on me now, throat!* she pleaded to herself, on the verge of tears, before finally speaking.

"I—I only slipped and fell! That's…that's all…!"

She might not have been able to accuse Caroline, but she could at least remove the blame from Lana. She appealed to Cyril with her whole heart.

"Nobody was at fault… It's…it was just me being clumsy! I'm sorry!" she finished, bowing her head.

"Wait a minute—!" exclaimed Lana, dissatisfied.

But Monica quickly cut her off. "So! Um, it's all…all fine now! I-I'm sorry for, um, causing such a scene…!"

Then, figuring that without the victim in the picture, the situation would dissolve, she dashed up the stairs, feet clomping against the steps, and left the scene.

* * *

After flying up the stairs, Monica paused to catch her breath—she was practically wheezing by this time. The sound of her teeth chattering was unbearable.

…It's all right. It's all right. If I endure it, if I don't say anything unnecessary, things will work out…

She brushed a little bit of dirt off her skirt hem from when she'd fallen down the stairs, then readjusted her gloves, which had wriggled out of place. For now, she wanted to focus on searching for the assassin who was after Felix. The flowerpot incident had clearly been premeditated. A true assassination attempt. As his bodyguard, she couldn't overlook it.

But why was the culprit after the prince…?

Felix and the others appeared to believe that an accomplice of Aaron O'Brien's, who had committed an injustice, was acting out of spite. That didn't sound quite right to Monica, though.

Aaron O'Brien had implied that he'd had an accomplice. Why, then, would that accomplice not have attempted to get rid of Aaron instead, to make sure he didn't talk?

It's like an incomplete equation, full of holes…

She needed more information to fill in the gaps. She told herself that for now, she simply needed to gather that info. When she reached the room she had been seeking—music room two on the fourth floor of the eastern building—she came to a stop.

She could hear the notes of a piano from within. Someone was playing inside. Would they get mad at her if she entered without asking? Still, she wanted to carry out her investigation as soon as possible.

After some internal conflict, she lightly knocked on the door, then opened it.

The music room was elegant, like a little salon, and had a fine-looking piano inside. The piano was an instrument for the upper classes—far removed from the reach of the commoners. Sitting at that piano, her fingers sliding over the keys, was a female student with blond ringlets. Judging by the color of the scarf at her collar, she was a third-year in the advanced course.

The girl stopped playing, then said to Monica without shifting her gaze, "I'm using this room at the moment. If you need something, please come back later."

"U-um, I'm sorry. The balcony, um… I, er, left something on it…"

The blond young lady simply flipped through her score, then said, almost as if to herself, "Make it quick, please."

Monica mumbled a word of thanks and rushed out onto the balcony. As she'd expected, there were a number of flowerpots there. They looked similar to the one dropped in the rear gardens, too.

…Three pots have been planted with things already, and…

Just one of the flowerpots was empty, and it was sitting upside down near the edge of the balcony. Monica squatted to look at it. She picked it up, but there was nothing inside. It really was just an empty flowerpot turned upside down.

Why would this flowerpot be upside down and the others right side up? she wondered, returning the pot to its original position. The upside-down pot was filthy, and the dirt got onto her gloves. She brushed some of it off, but the rest stuck fast. She'd have to wash her gloves as soon as she got back to her dorm room. She didn't have a spare pair.

Worrying about her dirty gloves, she looked over at the balcony railing. Since it was meant to prevent people from falling off, it was pretty high. Monica, being small and weak, would have had a difficult time trying to lift a heavy flowerpot over the railing to drop it from up here.

Wait. What if…?

Monica stood for a while in thought, and eventually the sounds of the piano ceased. Coming to, she looked back toward the music room. The female student who had been sitting at the piano was now looking at her, expression cold.

A closer look revealed the girl to be extremely pretty. Even Monica, who didn't have a good sense of the difference between attractive and unattractive, could tell she was quite the beauty.

As Monica flinched away from the force of her stunning features, the girl closed the piano lid and said, "I'm going back to class. I'd like to lock up."

"Oh, I-I'm sorry! I'll leave!"

Monica locked the door connecting the music room to the balcony. Then, as the pretty student was locking the piano, Monica timidly asked, "Um, is this room…usually locked?"

"In order to use one of the music rooms, you have to borrow a key from the teachers' office. To use this one, you would need to submit an application for music room two."

Monica quietly muttered her thanks, then hurried out of the music room.

The girl's amber eyes remained fixed on her back as it disappeared down the hallway.

* * *

The accounting records, nonsensical and messed up as they now were, had truly been Aaron O'Brien's parting gift to the student council. As Felix silently looked back over the heavily altered books, Elliott, who had been reviewing receipts, said conversationally, "We should make a bet. How long until the little squirrel admits defeat? I give her three days."

"You don't like her?"

It was true that he had little faith in Monica Norton, but Elliott's attitude toward her was obvious.

Elliott sniffed. "No, I don't. She's not a noble, no matter how you look at her... For her to attend this academy at all is conceit of the highest order." He spoke casually, but a very real distaste was evident in his voice. Looking over at Felix, he lowered his voice and said, "I can't stand commoners who don't know their place."

"Yes, I know."

Most of the girls who went to Serendia Academy were from noble families, but there were still plenty from the lesser nobility and below. Generally, as long as you could afford the tuition, you could enroll. But many, including Elliott, didn't think highly of this state of affairs.

"Still," remarked Felix, "don't you think you're being quite mean? Just how many classrooms face the rear gardens? I really doubt a new student like her would be able to investigate all of them."

"It's still better than us doing it and being noticed. And as for sneaking out of your room at night...well, that doesn't sound like the behavior of a prince."

Elliott's words were thorned as he narrowed his droopy eyes at Felix. He probably wasn't happy that Felix had acted alone.

But Felix parried his critical stare with a cool look and slid a feathered pen across the page in front of him. "I want to deal with all academy trouble in as secret a manner as possible. We don't want Duke Clockford intervening, after all."

Duke Clockford was Felix's maternal grandfather and one of the most influential nobles in the kingdom, and Serendia Academy was under his jurisdiction. If a major incident occurred here, it would be like rubbing dirt in the duke's face—something he could absolutely not allow. Even if others called him the duke's lapdog, Felix could never, ever disobey him.

"And most importantly... As Felix Arc Ridill, I can't have people thinking I lack the competence to handle such a situation."

As Elliott was about to respond, there came a soft knocking

from the student council room door. After calling out, "Please come in," the door slowly opened to reveal a small girl.

It was Monica Norton. The new second-year student in the advanced course. A scrawny girl, nothing about her—not her appearance or her behavior—fit the mold of the rest of Serendia Academy.

Feeling some pity for the girl after Elliott's bullying, Felix gently called out to her. "Hello, Lady Norton. Made any progress?"

It had been only a few hours, so progress was unlikely. Felix hadn't been expecting anything from the girl in the first place.

But this small girl—this brand-new student—fiddled with her fingers and said in a very, very quiet voice:

"I know...who the culprit is."

CHAPTER 7

The Second Prince's Secret

"Oh, Selma, how positively terrible that your fiancé, Aaron, should have to leave school!"

"A sudden illness? What a waste—he'd become student council accountant and everything."

"And he left you behind at the academy, too! I feel so sorry for you!"

Selma's friends whispered to her, with expressions that said they didn't feel the least bit sorry.

Friends... Yes, they were friends. Even if Selma had to suck up to them, even if she was the one who did all their errands, she could rest easy as long as she had people she could label *friends*. After all, her looks were plain and had no redeeming features. She had nothing—but if she had friends, then that was something.

"You know, I heard that Aaron was head over heels for Bridget, in third-year."

"Oh, when he's already engaged to Selma?!"

"I suppose one can't blame him—Lady Bridget is truly beautiful." Selma's friend, mouth hidden behind her fan, then added in a low voice, "Unlike plain-looking Selma."

Aaron O'Brien—he was a very precious fiancé for someone who had nothing. Even if Aaron didn't love her, he was still important to her. *That's why I have to help him*, she thought. *And that person said I was the only one who could...* Selma squeezed her hands into fists inside her brand-new gloves.

A moment later, her friends all looked up, their voices brightening. Selma followed suit and saw a young man with olive-brown hair looking at her—the student council secretary, Elliott Howard.

"Hi there, Lady Selma Karsh. I'm sorry to bother you during your valuable break time. Do you have a few moments?"

Ah, so it's time. Selma bit her lip and didn't say anything.

* * *

It was lunch break, several hours after Monica had ascertained the culprit behind the falling flowerpot. She was in the student council room waiting when Elliott returned with Selma Karsh in tow.

Selma was looking down and cowering, making her already small frame even smaller. It was the face of someone who knew why they were there. Her features were pale but filled with tragic resolve, her hazel eyes darkened.

Excluding Selma, the only three in the room were Felix, Elliott, and Monica. Selma's eyes darted questioningly to Monica for a brief moment. She was probably wondering why Monica was in the student council room.

"Now then."

With that short preface from Felix, the mood in the room changed at once. All he had done was let a tiny chill creep into his usually serene voice, and the tension around them pulled taut. Just a slight narrowing of his gentle blue eyes altered the character of his smile.

He could intimidate and command those around him with only his tone of voice and facial expression. That was what it meant to be royalty—Monica felt this keenly as she saw Selma shrink back.

"Two days ago, on the day before the entrance ceremony, a signboard at the venue fell down toward me. And yesterday, in the rear gardens, a flowerpot did as well. Very similar incidents. Most likely committed by the same person."

Felix's fingers tapped on the desk. That was all it took for Selma to nearly jump out of her skin.

"Lady Monica Norton here insists that you were behind both. Lady Norton, would you mind explaining your logic?"

Monica squeaked in surprise. She'd just informed Felix and Elliott of her investigation's results. She wished the prince would have explained instead, but she reluctantly began to speak.

"Um," she said, "the location of the signboard incident had already been cleaned up, so I had no way of investigating it, but... As for what balcony the flowerpot was dropped from... A look at where it landed and the way it shattered makes that relatively clear. The flowerpot was dropped from music room two on the fourth floor."

As Monica began to write equations on the blackboard to give a more concrete explanation, Felix cut her off.

"No need to go that far."

Ugh... But talking about equations is so much easier... Glumly putting the chalk down, she continued. "Once I knew what balcony it had been dropped from, the rest was simple. You have to submit an application to use music room two, so..."

"I verified it personally," said Elliott, glaring at Selma. "The only application to use music room two during lunch break yesterday was submitted under your name, Lady Selma Karsh."

Selma remained silent, eyes downcast. Monica chose her next words carefully.

"Next to the balcony railing, I found one dirty flowerpot placed upside down. This is because the culprit, someone short, used it as a stepping stool. The railing on that balcony is pretty high, so..."

The use of one flowerpot as a stepping stool and another, empty and thus lighter, flowerpot for the crime both spoke to the likelihood that the culprit was a petite girl without much physical strength. *And most importantly...*

Monica looked at Selma. She was wearing a pair of brand-new

white gloves. Gloves were part of the uniform at the academy, but when Monica had woken up in the infirmary, Selma hadn't been wearing them. Her fingers had been delicate and white—they were the hands of a maiden who had never known manual labor, and their image was still burned into Monica's memory.

The reason she hadn't been wearing gloves was because she'd gotten them dirty when she'd moved the flowerpot to use it as a stepping stool. The pot dropped from the balcony had been clean—only the one turned upside down was dirty. The reason Selma had flipped over the pot even if it meant getting her gloves dirty was because she had needed the added height.

"...I found a pair of dirt-stained gloves in the garbage bin of the powder room closest to music room two. Your initials were embroidered on them."

That was the final blow. Selma, who had already been looking down, dropped to her knees and covered her face with her hands. "Yes... Yes, it was me!" she cried, sobbing and lifting up her face. Her tear-soaked cheeks twitched as her lips formed a warped smile. Her eyes were wide now and unfocused. "I was the one who dropped the flowerpot and the signboard... And I was the one who embezzled the funds, too! I did everything! I pushed Aaron to do it! I deceived him every step of the way! So... Oh, please, I beg you, have mercy on him... He isn't at fault. I'll return all the money he embezzled!"

Felix watched with pity in his eyes as Selma pleaded desperately, then shook his head.

"Unfortunately, we already know Aaron O'Brien was involved in the embezzlement. Nothing you can say will overturn his sentence."

"Please... Please, I... You can do whatever you want with me... Just forgive him...," begged Selma through her sobs.

Elliott made a sour face. "Why would you go this far to protect Aaron? He was spending that money on other women. You're his fiancée."

The question was cruel, but Selma didn't seem shocked. She probably already knew that Aaron didn't love her. But she'd still borne a grudge against Felix for Aaron's sentence, had attempted to harm Felix, and in the end had tried to take all the blame for the embezzlement.

Had it been out of devotion? Or had she wanted that badly to win Aaron's heart? Monica couldn't tell.

Monica had been able to figure out that Selma was the culprit merely from examining the flowerpot shards. But no matter how many words were lined up in explanation, she couldn't understand the girl's feelings—of wanting Aaron to love her.

Selma's crimes had been very sudden and reckless. It was as if she didn't care if she was found out, as long as she could protect Aaron.

...*How can someone put that much faith in another?* thought Monica, looking at the girl impassively.

Felix then instructed Elliott to take Selma to a separate room. Eventually, she'd probably be given the same sentence as Aaron.

After Selma and Elliott had left the room, Monica glanced over at Felix. "Um...What's going to...to happen to her?"

"The signboard and flowerpot incidents were attempts to assassinate royalty. It's only reasonable that she and her entire family would be given the maximum possible penalty, don't you think?"

Felix's voice was calm but cold. Monica balled her hands in front of her chest and shuddered. She'd proven Selma's guilt and thus sentenced her and her entire family to death.

...*This is what it means to protect royalty.* Monica looked down, the color drained from her face.

At that, Felix softened his tone somewhat. "...That's what I would have said, at least, but making these incidents public would present a problem. The more appropriate thing to do in this situation would be to have her, too, willingly leave school due to health issues." He straightened up in his seat and sighed a little. "And more than that, the sight of her throwing away everything for someone import-ant to her...was rather moving."

His blue eyes seemed to look through Monica to someplace far away. Monica's brow furrowed, and she tilted her head to one side. "I–is that so?"

As she'd watched Selma try to throw her life away with no guar-antee of reward, Monica hadn't seen her behavior as noble—she had thought it was terrifying.

Monica understood attachment. But her attachment was to equations and magical formulas. She couldn't feel that attachment for people and so she couldn't understand Selma.

...I just don't really get it.

At any rate, the case had been closed, and thus suspicion toward Monica had been lifted. Figuring she could go back to class now, she glanced a few times at Felix.

"Then I'll, um, just be...going..."

But right as she said that, her eyes fell on the documents Felix had spread out on his desk. Judging by the dense lines of numbers on them, they were accounting records. The revision markings dot-ting the pages were probably corrections of items Aaron O'Brien had altered.

As she looked at all the numbers, she felt her pulse quicken with excitement. She was the type whose heart sang at the sight of pages filled with numbers, just like these accounting records.

...But the sparkle in Monica's eye soon dimmed. "...Three places," she murmured, eyeing the documents dubiously.

"I'm sorry?" said Felix, tilting his head.

Until now, Monica had been keeping plenty of distance between herself and Felix, but now she barged over to his desk, pointed at the papers, and said in an unusually firm tone, "Right here, and here, and here—the numbers aren't correct."

Monica loved beautiful equations. Just as others might cherish works of art for their beauty, Monica loved formulas. That was why seeing incomplete equations or fishy accounting records made her *very* irritated. Like stains on otherwise perfect works of art, miscalculations drove her mad.

And the documents in front of her were just *littered* with stains.

As Monica eyed the papers closely, Felix addressed her.

"Do you know how to read accounting records?"

"Only the central system and the western standard system, but yes...," answered Monica, staring only at the written numbers, without even glancing at Felix. Anyone would agree her behavior was an affront to royalty.

But rather than rebuke her, Felix's lips turned up in an amused smile. "Lady Norton, if it's all right with you, would you help review these records?"

Monica's head jerked away from the numbers, and she exclaimed, "May I?!"

The work that had piled up in her mountain cabin was being assigned by Louis Miller to other people, and her classes at Serendia Academy were mainly language, history, and culture.

To be blunt, Monica had been starved for numbers.

"Come here," said Felix, beckoning for her to follow him to the adjacent reference room. Inside were beautifully adorned locked shelves, each of which was packed full of string-bound documents. "In the back are the historical student records, next to those are current student records, and then those related to faculty. Records of events are over here."

Felix proceeded to explain the contents of each and every shelf before stopping in front of the one farthest to the right.

"And this is the shelf for accounting documents," he said, removing a ring of keys from his shirt pocket, unlocking the shelf, and removing some documents. The room contained a workstation with a desk and chair, and he placed the papers on the desk. "What I'd like to request from you is a review of our accounting records dating back five years."

"I...I understand!" answered Monica, unable to hide her jubilation.

"Thank you," Felix said with a winning smile.

Most noble girls would be enraptured by a smile like that, but Monica's wide eyes were already glued to the stack of papers before her.

"As for your classes," he continued, "I'll talk to your teachers. There's a lot of it, so just do what you can for now."

"I will!" she answered, already flipping through the ledgers.

Her eyes were sparkling—she hadn't been this excited in a long time.

* * *

...*Now then.*

Watching Monica's profile as she got to work on the ledgers, Felix—as naturally as he could—dropped his key ring from his pocket.

The girl didn't seem to notice the light *ching-ling* it made as it hit the floor. But he'd dropped it between the work desk and the shelf of documents, so she would be sure to see it when she got up. Then he left her alone in the reference room.

Once he was down the hallway and around a corner, he checked to make sure nobody was nearby, then gave his pocket a light tap. "Wildianu?"

At Felix's call, a small lizard slithered out of his pocket. The lizard's eyes were light blue, and his scales were white with a hint of that same light blue. No lizard had coloring like this, but this was no lizard—this was a high-ranking spirit contracted to Felix.

"Did you call, Master?"

Felix placed a hand next to his pocket, and Wildianu climbed up his finger and crawled onto the back of his hand. He brought the lizard close to his face and quietly commanded him, "Stay near the reference room and keep an eye on Lady Norton."

"...Is that why you purposely dropped the keys?"

Felix gave a quiet chuckle. This smile was different from his usual "princely" smile, which was calm and gentle. This was the smile of a hunter setting a trap.

Now that Monica had gotten close to him and asked to see their accounting records, Felix no longer believed her to be just some ordinary girl. He had to assume she had some goal in mind, and he could think of three possibilities.

The first possibility was that she'd been sent by Duke Clockford, his maternal grandfather, to keep an eye on him. The second was that she'd been sent by his father, the king, to keep an eye on him or to protect him. The third and final possibility was that she was an assassin after his life.

But for someone sent by Duke Clockford or the king, Monica was surprisingly incompetent. It was hard to imagine either of them would send someone so absentminded and careless.

Still, though, he was far from convinced that she was an assassin sent to kill him. She hadn't even appeared to know his face. And besides, if she was an assassin, she would have tried to harm him when he went out the night before.

From the back of Felix's hand, the white lizard hesitantly asked, "Isn't it possible that Lady Monica Norton truly is…just a girl?"

"That's why I'm testing her."

If Monica had come to this academy with an objective in mind, she was sure to fish around in the reference room—using the keys Felix had dropped.

"If Lady Norton picks up the keys and starts scavenging through bookshelves that don't have anything to do with her work, report it to me."

That was why Felix had told her which shelf was which to begin with.

"Understood, Master," said Wildianu before Felix gently lowered him to the floor.

"Let's wait, say, until classes end today. By that time, she'll have shown us her true colors."

"…And if she hasn't?"

At Wildianu's question, Felix narrowed his blue eyes and smiled. "Hmm. In that case…"

* * *

Each day after classes ended, people with places to go—those attending clubs, tea parties, and the like—had to move. Naturally, the hallways became packed.

Among the crowd were three female students standing and chatting by the student council room. At their center was Caroline Simmons, the caramel-haired daughter of Count Norn.

"Why was Selma called to the student council, I wonder?" said Caroline from behind her folding fan.

Her two followers kept their voices down as they replied.

"Perhaps something has happened with Aaron. She is his fiancée, after all."

"I doubt this would happen, but… She would never succeed him as the student council accountant, would she?"

Caroline snorted in amusement. To think—Selma, that boring, unappealing girl, a student council member!

Members of the student council were the elite of Serendia Academy. You couldn't be chosen unless you both came from an excellent family and had excellent grades—especially not with Felix Arc Ridill, second prince of the kingdom, as its current president.

King Ridill had three sons, but he hadn't yet announced who would inherit the throne. Currently, the movement supporting the second prince as the next king was gaining strength among the nobility. After all, he was the one with the backing of Duke Clockford, a major noble. The second prince's faction grew stronger by the day. If this state of affairs continued, he would surely inherit the throne.

That also meant that all the noble ladies at this academy were practically falling over one another to become his fiancée. All the more so as Felix was much, *much* more physically attractive than the boorish first prince or the young and forgettable third prince.

Caroline, who had fallen in love with Felix at first sight, loitered near the student council room every chance she got. With Felix being in his third year and Caroline in her second, they had few chances to encounter each other, even in the same school. She would have to create those opportunities herself.

Lord Felix should be coming down the hallway any minute, she thought, quietly determined. Today would be the day she would catch his eye.

Just then, she heard footsteps behind her. Her heart leaped in anticipation—could that be him? She turned around and saw, instead, a stunningly beautiful girl with sleek blond hair.

This was the only female student in the student council—Bridget Greyham, daughter of Marquess Shaleberry. She was also one of the three most beautiful girls at Serendia Academy. Turning her pretty face toward the other students, she said coldly, "You're blocking traffic. Could you move along?"

That was all it took to make Caroline's two followers look down in embarrassment and moved over to the wall. Caroline followed suit. If this were Lana Colette, that impudent nouveau riche girl, she'd probably have said, *Why don't you go around me?* Bridget, however, was on a completely different level.

Her grades were excellent, and she maintained a high rank even as a third-year. Especially when it came to linguistic fields—she was a genius rivaling even Felix, who held the highest-ranking grades overall. Neither her appearance nor her family lineage left anything to be desired, and she was Felix's childhood friend.

And above all, Bridget was the only female student Felix had nominated to the current student council. That alone showed the trust he'd placed in her, and many thought she was the most suited to be his fiancée.

She was an impeccable, perfect lady. In her presence, all Caroline could do was quietly look down and yield the way.

*　*　*

Bridget headed straight toward the student council room, without even so much as a glance at the girls standing outside. But when she turned the doorknob, her face scrunched up in suspicion. It was unlocked.

I was sure I'd be the first to arrive, she thought, a little confused, stepping into the room. She couldn't see anyone, but she could hear quiet sounds coming from the adjacent reference room. Thinking she would say hello to whoever was working, she peered into the room and was struck silent.

One of the shelves was empty, and stacks of paper were piled on the floor. At the desk in the back of the room, silently reading through the documents, was someone she hadn't expected to see there of all places—a girl with light-brown hair.

"You were in the music room earlier, weren't you? State your class and name. By whose permission have you entered this room?"

Despite Bridget speaking to her, the small girl didn't even give a start—or any reaction at all.

"Answer me," Bridget said more firmly. Still no response.

Growing impatient, Bridget was about to raise her voice even higher when two male students appeared behind her, both student council members.

"Oh? Lady Bridget got here first today, huh… Wait, what in the world?!"

"The documents have been left out everywhere! Wait—who is that?"

Both Elliott and Neil, the officer of general affairs, were shocked as they came up behind Bridget.

Elliott appeared to know the girl who had made a mess of the reference room, and he went up to the desk and addressed her.

"Lady Norton, what are you doing here? These are accounting records, aren't they? You shouldn't be looking at them without permission. Hey, Lady Norton. Lady Monica Norton, can you hear me?"

Despite Elliott's efforts, the girl whom he'd called Monica didn't seem to notice whatsoever. She continued reading through the accounting records without a word.

Neil furrowed his brow in worry. "By the looks of it, she's a second-year student like me... I haven't seen her before, though." He approached the desk and called to her from behind. "Hello? Excuse me? I'd like to talk to you. Do you have a moment?"

Still no answer as the girl flipped silently through page after page of the records. Sometimes, she would write a few numbers on a small slip of paper and place it between the pages. Her eyes never left those documents—never turned around to Bridget and the others.

As Elliott and Neil stood there at a loss, Bridget pushed past them and went up to the girl herself. Then she raised the folding fan in her hand and brought it down hard on the girl's cheek.

A loud *slap* echoed through the room, and the girl stopped for a moment. Elliott and Neil both recoiled, terrified at Bridget's behavior.

In the meantime, Bridget unfolded her fan and said coldly, "Awake now?"

"......"

The girl had stopped working for a few seconds, but eventually she started flipping through the pages again like nothing had happened.

* * *

That hurt.

Monica, her head lost in the world of numbers, suddenly felt a sharp pain in her cheek.

Things that hurt are scary. Scary things are hard to deal with.

The more pain and fear she felt, the more Monica's thoughts sank into the math.

After all, while she was thinking about numbers, everything was easy.

This beautiful world of numbers would never hurt her.

It would never say awful things and never cause her pain.

So when Monica felt the blow to her cheek, she turned ever further away from reality and plunged back into her equations.

* * *

Ack, this is really bad! Monica's completely out of control!

During his explorations of the school building, the black cat Nero had happened to spot this scene through the student council window. He'd witnessed it all—including when Monica had been slapped with the fan.

No, that won't work! Hitting her like that has the opposite effect! If you make Monica scared right now, she'll only become harder to reach!

Nero knew how to return her to her senses. The answer was his paws. If he squished her cheeks with his paws, she'd come to. He wanted to go to her, but the window was locked, and he couldn't get inside. He scratched at the window, meowing.

The smallest boy was the first to notice Nero. "Oh, a cat," he said. The other two followed his gaze to the window.

Great! Here we go!

Nero gently settled on the window frame, striking his cutest pose and giving a nice "meow."

How do you like my secret technique?! I've put everything into this alluring pose! It makes all the little girls go absolutely crazy for me! When he posed like this, most humans would be charmed instantly and let him inside.

You can feel free to groom me and give me food, too! thought Nero, snorting proudly.

The young lady with the folding fan said flatly, "I hate creatures who are only good at sucking up to others."

Mew, mew... Mew—what?!

Nero flew into a rage. How could he tolerate this? The answer was that he couldn't. This was absolutely unacceptable. He was way too cute to be treated this way!

Which one of you just called me a creature who's only good at sucking up?! Try saying that to my face! I'll show you what happens when I mean business.

Nero stamped his feet and meowed angrily, but Monica still didn't notice him. As he thought, the only way to get her to snap out of it was to squeeze her cheeks with his paws.

Let! Me! In! Let me squish her cheeks!

As Nero scratched frantically at the window, another two people entered the reference room.

It was the second prince and student council president and a silver-haired boy who appeared to be his aide.

The second prince, his golden locks glittering, glanced around the reference room.

"Hi there," he said. "What's all the ruckus about?"

* * *

The first thing Felix did upon entering the reference room was check the key ring.

...It's still where I dropped it.

Casually, he glanced over at the other shelves, but there were no signs of tampering. The only one that had been completely ransacked was the shelf that held the accounting records.

Wildianu, the lizard who had snuck into the room to keep an eye on Monica Norton, crawled up Felix's clothes. Eventually, when he had reached Felix's shoulder, he said, softly enough not to be overheard by the others, "All she's been doing for hours, ever since lunch break, is reviewing those records."

"...Hmm."

Felix picked up some of the papers at his feet and gave their contents a look. They were accounting records from twenty-four years ago, with small slips of paper indicating the corrected figures. The other documents were the same.

As he was looking them over, Vice President Cyril stared at Monica with suspicion. "I remember you from the staircase incident earlier... What are you doing here?"

"Staircase incident? Cyril, are you acquainted with Lady Norton?" asked Felix.

Cyril stammered out a vague "w-well, sort of" and nodded.

Monica showed no reaction to this exchange, either. She continued silently working.

That was when Felix suddenly noticed the swelling on Monica's right cheek. "What is this?" he asked.

"A little punishment from me to someone who is being *very* rude," answered Bridget with a straight face before concealing her mouth with her fan.

So Monica's attitude had irritated Bridget. With gloved fingertips, he lightly brushed Monica's cheek. But once again, she didn't even blink.

"I asked her to do a review of our accounting records," he explained to the others, doing some mental arithmetic on a page with a correction slip.

Her correction was right on the mark—there was a defect.

...*Then she's going through* all *the past records?* Even Felix couldn't help but be surprised. How long had it been since something had surprised him this much?

Feeling a twinge of admiration, Felix softly tapped Monica on the shoulder. "Lady Norton, excellent work. You can take a break now."

Monica didn't answer him.

"Lady Norton?" Felix shook her shoulder a little bit more firmly, but Monica raised her right arm—and of all things, brushed his hand away in annoyance.

This sent a stir through the other council members. Cyril, who had sworn an oath of loyalty to Felix, was especially angry—enraged, even. Veins appeared on his temples, and he began to spread ice mana. Cyril was generally a very polite young man when it came to the female students, but if someone harmed Felix, that was a different story.

"You *wretch*! How dare you act so rudely toward His Royal Highness! You deserve to be *hung*!" he raged, starting to chant a spell.

Felix held a hand up to stop him. Monica was focusing every ounce of attention she had on doing her calculations. The girl who had been so fidgety and nervous trying to judge his reactions wasn't even looking at him any longer.

A hint of curiosity began to tickle his heart, and a thin smile appeared on his lips. He stroked Monica's face with a finger, then gave her a little peck on her swollen cheek.

As the other council members looked on in silent shock, Monica suddenly stopped moving—but her eyes remained on the documents.

"...Nero, just a minute... I'm almost done..."

"Nero?" repeated Felix, tilting his head to the side.

Monica's thin shoulders suddenly gave a start, and the feather pen fell from her hand. Soon, she began to tremble all over, lifting up her small face to look at Felix.

"P-P-P-P-Pri-Prin-Pr-Pri-Pri..."

"Yes. That's more like it." Felix laughed brightly at Monica's strange stammering.

Monica fell from her chair and proceeded to prostrate herself on the floor.

"I'm, I'm so, so, sor-sorr— Ack!" She must have bitten her tongue at the end. She held her mouth and started whimpering. "If furts."

Enjoying the chance to watch such a strange and delightful creature, Felix gently patted her head. "You can look up, all right? You did your best to fulfill my request, didn't you? You didn't do anything wrong."

"Eep... Y-yeffir—" Monica nodded, sniffling loudly.

"Um, sir," interrupted Elliott. "Sir, you ordered this little squirrel to review the records?"

"Yes. I asked her to look over the last five years, but… Even I didn't expect her to go through *all* our past records in just a few hours." Felix paused, then smiled at Monica, who was still sniffling. "Lady Norton, what did you think when you looked at those accounting records?"

"U-um… Well…"

"You can be honest with me. I won't be angry," he encouraged her, voice calm.

Monica began to fiddle with her fingers. "…A surprising amount of money is being moved around, and yet, its management is surprisingly sloppy, which, um, surprised me."

"How *dare* you!" screamed Cyril.

Monica put her hands over her head. "You said you wouldn't get mad…," she whimpered.

Another thin smile appeared on Felix's lips as he looked around at the other student council members. "This is the state of our student council's long history. Even I wasn't able to immediately identify Aaron O'Brien's misdeeds… And so, reflecting on past mistakes, I would like to make a declaration." He then took Monica's hand as she continued to sob and cower, loudly proclaiming, "I hereby appoint the second-year advanced-course student Lady Monica Norton as student council accountant."

A moment later, Monica's eyes rolled back, and she fainted on the spot.

All the while, the black cat outside the window continued loudly meowing.

* * *

"Hey, Monica, wake up. Hey!"

Monica could hear Nero's voice. She could feel the softness of his paw squishing her cheek.

Monica's eyes cracked open, and she realized she was lying on a simple bed. The bed was surrounded by curtains intended to isolate it, and she could smell the faint scent of disinfectant.

She remembered the ceiling above her. This was the infirmary she'd been brought to after the flowerpot incident.

Rolling over in bed, she saw Nero seated at her side. Animals were forbidden in the infirmary, so he'd probably snuck in through a window.

"...Nero, listen to this. I just had an incredible dream. I dreamed I was made student council accountant..."

"Listen and be amazed, Monica, for that was no dream—that was real!" said Nero, poking Monica's collar with his front leg.

An unfamiliar decorative pin now adorned her lapel. It was the same one Felix and the other student council members wore—proof that she was a council member.

Monica sat up in bed and fixed her eyes on the pin. "Wh-wha-what is this...?!"

"That sparkly prince put it on your collar. Humans really like this stuff, eh? Showing off their authority and all that." Nero nodded to himself, then pummeled Monica in the thigh with his paws. "Either way, you've done an excellent job. Now you can stay near the prince as a student council member."

"Y-yes, well... But..."

Considering her mission to secretly guard the second prince, her appointment as accountant was something to celebrate...but for an uninteresting girl like her to be chosen as a student council member? Few would be pleased with that.

At the time, Monica had been practically crawling on the floor, so she hadn't seen the council members' faces. But even from down there, she could feel their cold, hostile gazes. Especially from the vice president, Cyril Ashley. He'd seemed ready to use an offensive spell or two on her.

"Th-they're going to bully me for sure... Ugh... They're going to put thumbtacks in my shoes, and hide my pencils, and pour water on my uniform... I can't; I don't want to go back to class anymore..."

"Oh! I've read about things like that in novels! You mean people actually *do* that stuff?"

"Why does it sound like you're enjoying this?!" cried Monica bitterly.

Just then, Nero's ears perked up. "Hey, Monica, someone's coming," he said, quickly scooting under the bed to hide.

Who could it be? A nurse? thought Monica as the curtains surrounding the bed were pushed aside.

But it was no nurse—it was Felix.

Reflexively, she pulled her blanket over her head. She was fully aware that it was rude, but her hands had moved on their own. She couldn't help it. It was a defensive instinct.

Felix didn't seem unhappy about it, though. In fact, he grinned, apparently amused. "Oh, you're up? Sorry for not saying something. I figured you were still asleep."

"N-no, I, y-y-y-you d-d-do..."

"I do?"

"You don't, um, need to...mention it...," Monica squeezed out, using all her effort.

"I see," said Felix, evidently entertained. Then, of all things, he sat on the edge of her bed and crossed his legs.

Wanting to create as much distance as possible between them, Monica, still wrapped in the blanket, moved herself right to the edge of the bed...then lost her balance and fell off.

"Eek!"

Thankfully, her blanket prevented any real damage. But she had sure been falling a lot today.

As she sat sniffling on the floor, Nero looked at her from under the bed as if to ask what in the world she was doing. At this point, she just wanted to hide under the bed in her blanket.

Felix addressed her yet again. "A little squirrel, wrapping herself in a blanket... Are you going into hibernation for the winter?"

"Y-yes, th-th-that's right, um, today, well, it was, um, very c-cold, so..."

Summer had just given way to autumn, and the weather was extremely comfortable. Nevertheless, Monica gripped her blanket and heroically insisted she was cold.

Then Felix put his hand over Monica's, still holding the blanket, and said, "Oh? You poor thing. We'll have to warm you up, then."

Monica immediately let go of the blanket, stood up, and jumped back and away from Felix...but she wasn't used to such movements and tripped over her foot, falling back to the floor with a funny-sounding yelp.

Once again, her eyes met Nero's under the bed. She wanted to cry. But she couldn't scrabble around on the floor forever. She slowly sat back up, hid herself behind the bed, and looked at Felix. "U-um, Y-Your Royal, um..."

"Feel free to call me President or even simply Felix. I don't mind. You're my fellow council member now, after all."

Felix's words forced Monica to face reality.

She plucked the decorative pin off her lapel and said to Felix, body shaking, "Th-the role of accountant is, um...too much for me... sir."

"Not happy with my leadership?"

Simply by letting a tiny bit of a chill creep into his voice, he was suddenly a *lot* more intimidating. Monica shook her head so hard, she felt like it might pop off.

Felix smiled and said, "Then there's no problem, is there?" and took Monica's hand. He turned it faceup, then pressed something into it. It was a baked treat with plenty of berries on top. "Your reward for today. You did a good job."

"I, th-thank... Mgh!"

As Monica tried to thank him, he stuffed the treat into her mouth. Realizing she had skipped lunch, she began chewing it without speaking. It was a cookie—a little hard, with berries stuck onto it with honey. She'd never had anything like it before. It was *very* tasty.

Once she began eating, Monica was the type to focus on her meal until finished. For this reason, she forgot that she'd just requested to leave her accountant post and simply gnawed on the cookie, taking in its flavor.

"Is it good?" asked Felix, sounding amused.

Monica nodded at him, her mouth full of cookie.

He placed another in her hand, then quietly rose. "If you continue to do well, there's more where that came from," he said. "See you tomorrow."

Felix waved his hand and left the infirmary.

Alone now, Monica swallowed the rest of the cookie, then finally snapped out of her trance. "Ahhhh! I missed my chance to refuse the accountant position!" she wailed. "What am I supposed to do now, Nero?!"

"You know… You don't sound very convincing with that snack in your hand."

Monica sniffled, then put the cookie in her pocket.

Oh, right…, she thought. She brought her hand up to her swollen cheek and then looked at Nero, expression serious. "Nero, listen. I accidentally learned a huge secret about the prince."

"Ooh? And what's that? His weakness?" asked Nero, wagging his tail left and right, eyes sparkling.

Monica nodded gravely and said, "The prince……………… ………………………has paws."

Nero said flatly, "No, he doesn't."

"B-but in the reference room! I felt a paw pad squish my cheek, and then I came to and saw him," she insisted, rubbing her cheek.

Nero's expression suddenly went serious. "Just forget about it, Monica. Understand? Forget about all of that."

"Huh? Um, okay."

* * *

Once Felix had returned to his dorm room, Felix's white lizard, Wildianu, crawled up out of his uniform pocket. As the lizard landed on the floor, a pale mist enveloped him, and he transformed into a young man with hair the same color as the lizard's scales. His features were handsome enough, but he seemed somehow forgettable and lacking in ambition. He wore a neat, well-fitted servant's uniform. His hair was inhumanly white with hints of blue, and he wore it combed back.

Now in human form, the spirit Wildianu bowed reverently, then removed Felix's vest and hung it up. He asked, somewhat hesitantly, "Was this wise, Master?"

It was obvious what Wildianu was getting at—Monica Norton's appointment as accountant. Felix took a seat on the sofa and gave a slight shrug. "She didn't touch the reference room keys I purposely dropped. You were watching her, right? I can't think of any reason to criticize her."

After Monica had passed out, he'd taken a look through all the records—and every single one of the things she'd pointed out had been correct. Seventy-four years of records, and Monica had reviewed them all within a matter of hours. Her mathematical abilities were perfectly suited for an accountant's work.

"Of course, I don't believe she's just some girl," said Felix. "I'm sure she had a reason to come into contact with me."

At the moment, Felix didn't know which faction Monica Norton belonged to or her objective for getting close to him. Still, he was certain there was *something* about her. As he reclined on the sofa, he tilted his head just slightly and looked up at Wildianu. "You're probably wondering why I made her accountant despite all that, right?"

"...Yes, sir. You also noticed former accountant Aaron O'Brien's misdeeds from the beginning, didn't you?"

Felix had let the boy do as he pleased for a year, since just one or two times wouldn't have warranted severe punishment. He had to be sure he could drive Aaron O'Brien from the academy.

"And after you'd finally managed to have him expelled...why did you make her his successor?"

Felix didn't answer his servant's question immediately. Instead, he reached for the chessboard he'd left out on the low table. He plucked a white pawn from the board and let it roll around in his palm. "It's a game, Wil."

"...A game, sir?"

"Yes. A game where I try to tame a little squirrel and get her to confess what she's up to." He set the pawn back onto the board and narrowed his eyes, enjoying himself. "You saw her, too. She had no interest in me at all. She seems to think 'Old Man Sam's Pigs' is more impressive."

"W-well, sir, that's..."

Monica had been so engrossed in the documents that she hadn't spared Felix a single glance. And then, when he'd closed the distance in the infirmary, she had gone pale as a sheet and fallen out of bed. She wasn't trying to hide her embarrassment, either—no, she had felt genuine fear.

"But with the selection for the throne so close at hand, are such games truly—?"

"Wildianu," interrupted Felix in a singsong voice; Wildianu straightened up. "My life only lasts until the next king is selected. Why not...let me have a little fun?"

He lifted his eyebrows just slightly and offered an ephemeral smile.

Wildianu, who knew Felix's desire, politely bowed at the waist. "As you command, my lord."

Felix nodded in satisfaction, then moved the white queen to the edge of the chessboard. "Still, though, sneaking out for some nighttime enjoyment yesterday was a mistake. To think Lady Norton would see me... I covered it up by saying it was a decoy operation, but still."

The reason Felix had been outside the night before hadn't actually been to uncover the one behind the assassination attempts. He'd slipped out to have some time away from the dorm—and hadn't told Elliott about it.

"The little squirrel is surprisingly sharp-eyed... I should probably refrain from nighttime excursions for the time being."

"Perhaps you should put an end to them altogether, sir."

"Well, I suppose I'll have to think of ways to lure in the little squirrel to pass the time instead."

Felix chuckled, then flicked over the white pawn. It rolled across the board, then fell.

Very much like how Monica had rolled off the bed.

CHAPTER 8
Eyelash Mechanics

"Argh, I swear… What is the prince thinking?" muttered Cyril Ashley as he looked over the documents from the reference room.

Felix hadn't ordered him to carry out a review. The other student council members had already returned to their dorms. Cyril had taken it upon himself to stay and look through them because he couldn't bring himself to trust Monica Norton.

The prince had said she'd reviewed all past documents, but there was no way she could have done that in the few hours between lunch break and the end of classes. It must have been a mistake—and so Cyril was in a frenzy, searching for any signs that Monica had done a sloppy job.

Unfortunately, the more he reviewed, the more he came to realize that Monica's review had been perfect. She'd pointed out very minor numerical mistakes that even Cyril would have overlooked. At this point, he had to acknowledge her ability for calculations was incredible, but…

"…I still don't like it."

How dare that girl ignore Felix—the second prince himself—when he was speaking to her and look at documents instead! It was a slight against royalty!

He grew irritated, recalling the scene. But as he was cleaning up the papers, he suddenly noticed something.

…The numbers, they're written like…

All those imperfections Monica had discovered—he got the feeling they'd increased after a certain year.

And Cyril had an idea as to whose handwriting it was on the added lines. The numbers were written with a rightward slant—very common for a left-handed person.

…Could it be? No, but wait, that's not…

Cyril checked the documents several more times, then stood up without a word. He needed an answer to this question. With the documents in hand, he left the student council room and headed for…

"……?"

In front of the student council room door, Cyril came back to his senses. What had he just been doing?

Oh, right. I needed to lock up and go return the council room key to Mr. Thornlee. The key was in his hand. But as he looked down at it, he felt something was off.

He hadn't been holding a key but some sort of documents. Then he remembered—yes, something about the documents had caught his eye, and so he'd…

"……"

Suddenly, his head started to sting. Cyril put a hand to his temple and leaned against the wall. He must have been tired. He'd probably zoned out because of that.

…Maybe I should go to sleep early tonight.

Still holding his throbbing head, he started walking toward the faculty room.

* * *

"What is the meaning of this?! How could *you*, the shame of our family, become a student council member?! I want the truth right now! How did you manage to ingratiate yourself to the prince?!"

The one shouting was Isabelle Norton, noble daughter of Count Kerbeck. Her voice resounded both through the room *and* down the hallway. Then she threw her teacup to the floor. The sound of the porcelain shattering made Monica gasp in fear.

Isabelle then picked up a stuffed animal at her bedside, swung it around, and slammed it into the wall. *Bumph, bumph* came the muffled noises.

"And just *what* is that defiant expression?! I see you don't understand your position here! In that case, I'll have to remind you of your place!" said Isabelle, slamming the stuffed animal into the wall with all her strength.

Then, with a refreshed expression, she wiped the sweat off her brow. Her face was filled with accomplishment, like a craftsman who had just finished a job.

"How was that for a villainess?" she asked.

"Um, u-um…," stammered Monica.

Then Isabelle's maid Agatha, who had been cleaning up the broken teacup, smiled and nodded. "That was wonderful, Lady Isabelle! You played the part to perfection!"

"Didn't I? Didn't I?! That last line—'I'll have to remind you of your place'—that was from the latest book!"

"Eee! Yes, I remember that! The count's daughter lifts her fork, intending to injure the heroine's face, and then the prince swoops in and saves her!"

"That's the scene! It was just so, *so* wonderful!"

Monica, who couldn't keep up with the excited chatter between Isabelle and her maid, took a tiny sip of the black tea they'd prepared for her. "U-um… Actually breaking the teacup, it seemed…like a little much…," she stammered, glancing at the remaining fragments.

Isabelle puffed out her chest. "That's no problem at all. In fact, it was already cracked! I stocked up on defective dinnerware for this exact purpose!"

"I… I see…"

"The key is to get the sound to echo, so instead of using a rug, I have to throw it onto a hard floor!"

As Isabelle detailed her pointlessly elaborate performance,

Agatha gave a full smile and clapped her hands. "Simply wonderful, my lady! You're a true performer!"

The night of her appointment as student council accountant, Monica had gone to her coconspirator Isabelle's room and filled her in on the development. She had figured since they were on this mission together, it would be best to share information.

But as soon as she had shared the news, Isabelle practically jumped into the air, as excited as if she'd been appointed herself, and quickly invited Monica to a tea party in celebration.

The affluent Isabelle not only had her own private room but three maids with her. The youngest was Agatha, who was apparently her reading buddy. She was happily cooperating with Isabelle's pretend villainess act, as well.

I-is she really fine with her own mistress playing the villain?

Monica could not understand how they were both having so much fun with this.

Anyone who happened to pass by this room would get the mistaken impression that Isabelle was chastising or punishing her. Wouldn't that lower Isabelle's reputation?

Paying this no mind, Isabelle returned the stuffed animal to its original location, then sat herself back down in an extremely elegant manner.

"Now then," she began. "Monica, my sister, congratulations on your new post as student council accountant. To be chosen for the council within just two days of enrolling is... Oh, I knew you were special!"

As Isabelle put a hand to her cheek and chattered excitedly, Agatha shot a glance toward the hallway and put her finger to her lips. "My lady, shh! They'll hear you out in the hallway if you're too loud."

"Oh! Yes, that's right. Then please excuse my whispering... Really, though, congratulations. I am as happy as if it had happened to me."

Monica, pointlessly toying with her cup, said in a weak voice, "Thank you…"

Isabelle gracefully brought her cup to her lips and took another sip of black tea before offering an elegant smile. Her behavior now, and her tasteful smile, seemed to belong to a completely different person than the one who had just been swinging that stuffed animal around.

"My sister, should anything at all trouble you during your time here at the academy, you need only tell me. While I may be acting as the villainess and doing a magnificent job at impeding you, I will always be supporting you from the shadows."

Impeding me but supporting me? What is that supposed to mean…? thought Monica, nodding vaguely. Isabelle's reaction to the news had already given her a headache, but her classmates would be a much more serious issue. If they learned that *she* had joined the student council, what would they do to her? She started trembling, even though it wasn't cold, and sipped more of her tea.

Isabelle's eyes stopped on Monica's head. "Come to think of it, your hair… It's different from when I saw you before."

"Um, this is… A girl in my class, um, did it for me…"

"Well, it's very cute. And it suits you well! …Agatha, please style my hair to match!"

"We can't do that," chided Agatha with a smile at Isabelle's plea. "The villainess can't match her hairstyle to that of the girl she torments, as if they were friends."

Isabelle groaned, disappointed. "Well then, in that case, let's do it on a holiday, when nobody is watching!"

"Yes, my lady. When the time comes, I shall do my utmost to give both of you adorable matching hairstyles."

Excited, Isabelle exclaimed, "Then it's a promise!"

As she watched their exchange, Monica thought about Lana. Isabelle had been overjoyed at her appointment as accountant, but that was because Isabelle was her coconspirator. Most people would think she was acting far above her station, wouldn't they? Even Lana,

SERENDIA ACADEMY
FIRST-YEAR
Isabelle Norton

who had braided her hair—if she found out about the appointment, would she come to hate Monica for showing off?

...I don't want that.

From the perspective of her mission, Monica should have been overjoyed at becoming a council member. She kept telling herself that. But when she imagined Lana glaring at her with cold eyes, she didn't feel happy in the slightest.

* * *

Just as she had expected, the day after she was appointed student council accountant, Monica was showered with curious looks from the moment she left her dorm room. Eyes followed her from the hallway into the classroom—it seemed the news had already made the rounds.

As she sat down in her seat and started pointlessly rearranging her writing utensils, she thought back to the events of the previous day.

Yesterday had been tumultuous to say the least. Elliott had summoned her, then ordered her to find the culprit behind the flowerpot incident. While on that mission, she'd fallen down the stairs and met a beautiful girl in the music room. And then, once she'd figured out who had dropped the flowerpot and joyfully reviewed the student council's accounting records, she had somehow wound up being named the council's new accountant.

As the one charged with Felix's protection, becoming accountant had been an amazing stroke of luck. But with how much she hated standing out, Monica just couldn't be happy about it.

Up until today, her classmates had seen her as a country bumpkin, and their stares had been ones of derision. But now she could plainly see the shift to envy and malice. The hatred stabbed into her skin like knives. Whispered voices were colored by irritation and ridicule.

I want to go home..., she thought, half crying, until all of a sudden, someone tapped her shoulder. Monica nearly jumped out of her skin and started trembling. She was too scared to turn around. She was probably being called out. Whoever it was would ask to speak with her behind the school building and then pour water all over her... She'd almost started crying when the person gave a yank on her braid.

"Hey. So it's back to your old hairstyle again?"

It was Lana, glaring at her with discontent. She had all her makeup on today, as always, with intricately styled hair and colorful hair ornaments.

Monica, on the other hand, had been so depressed about coming to school that morning that she'd had no motivation at all to practice the new hairstyle. At times like this, she got even sloppier about her appearance, and her braids were more disheveled than usual.

Seeing Lana frown in displeasure, Monica immediately apologized. "I'm—I'm sorry, I just... I couldn't practice like I, um, wanted to, and..."

"Does it have to do with getting taken to the student council room yesterday?"

"......"

"I heard a rumor that you'd become a student council member. That's a joke, right?"

Monica had removed the pin signifying her status as a council member and put it in her pocket. Her hand unconsciously moved to press against it through the cloth.

Lana puffed up her lips in a pout. "What? Don't want to talk to me anymore?"

"N-no... No! It's... I, well..."

As Monica mumbled, eyes downcast, Lana continued to stare at her. Monica was certain she'd made her unhappy, and she sat there in quiet depression.

Then Lana suddenly spoke up. "...I, well, yesterday..."

"Huh?"

"I wasn't the one who pushed you or anything, but I *was* the one who provoked Caroline, so... I'm, er... You're not...hurt, are you?"

Oh, right. Monica remembered. She'd been caught up in an argument between Caroline and Lana yesterday and had ended up falling down the stairs. To be honest, between investigating crimes and reviewing all those accounting books, she'd completely forgotten about it. But it seemed to have been on Lana's mind the entire time.

"...Thank...thank you. Um, I'm not...hurt. I'm just fine."

Lana gave a "hmph." Her cheeks were just a little red. As if to distract from it, she pushed up her flaxen hair and took out a comb. "Well, we can't leave you looking like this. I'll have to fix your hair again."

"...Heh-heh."

"What are you laughing about?! Hurry up and learn for yourself!"

"...Yes. I will." Monica nodded, feeling oddly happy.

"Oh? So your friend did your hair yesterday, huh?"

The voice was soft and sweet, and Monica had heard quite enough of it yesterday.

Lana froze in surprise. And it wasn't just her—everyone else in the classroom was focused on the newcomer as well.

Monica finally turned around, face stricken, and locked eyes with Felix, who stood there smiling. His soft blond hair glittered in the morning sun, and his blue eyes seemed filled with mystery. The girls in class all started squealing over his handsome features.

The more discriminating among them didn't make any noise but still looked at him with enraptured, passionate gazes. Lana was no exception—though she was shocked, Felix's beauty had charmed her as well.

"Morning."

"Good...g-good mrowning—mph!"

"Sorry for barging in so early like this. I wanted to give you a copy of the student council member schedule."

Felix's words sent a stir through their surroundings. Even Lana looked at Monica, eyes wide.

...I want to disappear.

Monica's face resembled that of a corpse as Felix handed her a piece of paper with the schedule written on it, then took his finger and ran it along her collar. "Oh? Where is your pin? Did you take it off?"

"Oh, um, uh…"

Monica turned her head to the side to avoid the question, but he took her chin and forced her to look straight ahead. "Why not take it out?"

Terrified, she took out her council member pin. He plucked it from her hand, then personally affixed it to her collar. "You have to keep it on, all right? You're a member of the prestigious student council, so you must always look the part."

Ah, I don't want to be on the student council. But for this bodyguard mission, I have to.

Still, the stares from those around her were so painful.

…I'm scared!

And now Felix was right next to her—way too close. To try and escape from reality, she started counting his eyelashes. *One, two, three, four…* His eyelashes were a slightly deeper color than his hair and startlingly long. How many matchsticks could sit across them? *Two… No, you might even be able to get three on there.*

As she counted the eyelashes, she simultaneously started thinking about how many lashes would be needed to support the weight of a matchstick. The strength of each individual lash, their relative density, and their angle were all important.

As she became lost in her escapist fantasy, the long eyelashes in front of her lifted, and those blue eyes flashed mischievously. "You're staring quite a lot. Why is that?"

"…M-m-m-matchsticks…"

"Hmm?"

"I was thinking about the optimal eyelash angle for supporting a matchstick!"

Every one of her classmates, who had been watching the scene with bated breath, suddenly froze. Lana paled and began stammering, "Wait, n-no… You—you foolish…"

But Felix only chuckled, his shoulders bobbing, and released Monica's collar. "You should have your friend do your hair—it was very cute yesterday. The ribbon suited you well." He lightly stroked her hair with a finger, then gave her a wink. "I'll see you after school. In the student council room."

Leaving her with that, Felix exited the classroom. Monica looked down and let out a long breath. She was tired. It was only morning, and she was already so tired. She wanted to go back to her room right now and hide under the covers...

As Monica was thinking that, Lana took out various combs and hairpins and laid them on the desk. Her eyes were practically sparkling.

"U-um...?" said Monica, frightened, looking up at Lana.

Huffing excitedly, Lana readied her combs. "My skills have been acknowledged by the prince... I can't send you to him with anything less than a masterpiece... Prepare yourself, for I am about to give you the number one cutest hairstyle trending in the capital!"

Monica was honestly overjoyed that Lana didn't hate her now that she was a student council member—but she was also a little scared of the fire blazing in her eyes as she held those combs.

"I'll take the one from yesterday, please!" exclaimed Monica as their teacher, Mr. Victor Thornlee, entered the classroom.

For a moment, she thought she saw him glare at her from behind his glasses. Monica was especially sensitive to the malice of others, and her shoulders shook at the feeling. Mr. Thornlee averted his eyes, then fussily tapped on the lectern.

"Everyone, take your seats," he said. "I have an announcement. A student from our class, Lady Selma Karsh, has returned home due to a sudden illness."

The classroom began to murmur. It was still fresh in everyone's memories how Aaron, Selma's fiancé, had left school for the same reason. A few girls particularly prone to gossip began speculating with abandon:

"Wasn't she really depressed about what happened to Aaron?"

"It couldn't have been attempted suicide, right?"

"Oh no, how terrifying!"

Mr. Thornlee cleared his throat. After looking around at the students, he continued. "As such, I will be selecting a new class health officer to take her place."

While she listened to Mr. Thornlee, Monica was thinking to herself. *So they really are keeping the truth a secret from her classmates... But then, why...?*

A little question bloomed in her mind. Their goal was to bury the academy's scandal so that none of the students, save the council, would ever know about it.

Then why had Selma Karsh known about Aaron O'Brien being convicted for his misdeeds?

Aaron O'Brien had been out of his mind when they'd taken him away, and Selma Karsh had been in a similar state when she'd insisted on Aaron's innocence. Their actions simply didn't add up, and it made Monica awfully curious.

* * *

Classes had ended for the day, and Monica was standing in front of the door to the student council room. Once again, she checked over her appearance. Her uniform was fine, her gloves were fine, and her hair had been properly re-braided by Lana.

She took a deep breath, in and out, then raised her hand to knock on the door...and lowered it back to her side again. She'd been doing the same thing over and over for some time now. That was the tenth deep breath she'd taken so far.

Standing in front of the door, taking deep breath after deep breath—she was the very image of a "suspicious person." It was her mission to eliminate all suspicious people near the second prince, but sadly, the most suspicious one was her.

Okay. This time. This time..., she thought, firming up her resolve and raising her hand again.

"Ummm, are you all right?" came a voice from behind her.

Monica was so startled that she leaped forward, smacking her forehead against the door. *Owww*, she thought, holding her forehead and shaking.

The owner of the voice bowed apologetically. "Oops! I'm sorry for surprising you like that. Um, you were standing there for a long time, just breathing, so I thought maybe you weren't feeling well..."

The speaker was a boy with light-brown hair. He was a little on the short side and seemed young, but his scarf's color indicated he was in the same year as Monica. And like her, he wore a student council pin on his lapel.

...He's a council member, too?

Come to think of it, she did remember several people in the reference room the day before. However, she'd been so absorbed in the numbers that she'd barely looked at anything else. She started to fidget.

The boy gave an elegant bow befitting a noble. "You're Monica Norton—our new accountant, right? I'm Neil Clay Maywood, the officer of general affairs. Pleased to meet you. We're the only second-years on the council, so I hope we can get along."

Neil followed up with a bashful smile—clearly, he was a good-natured person. *That's a relief*, thought Monica, quietly breathing a sigh. Deep down, she'd been terrified the other council members would hate her, but here was someone nice already. *Maybe I'll be able to do this after all...*, she thought, relieved.

At that exact moment, they heard an angry exclamation from behind them. "How long are you going to be talking in front of the door?!"

Monica's shoulders jerked. She turned around and saw the silver-haired Cyril Ashley, vice president of the student council, crossing his arms and glaring at her. He tipped his slender chin up into the air, stared, then said bitterly, "Monica Norton. Have you noticed that your prolonged nonsense is keeping me from getting inside?"

Apparently, Cyril had seen her taking all those deep breaths in front of the door.

"Um, Vice President...," ventured Neil. "Were you watching this whole time?"

Cyril turned his glare on Neil, and the boy, who seemed weak-willed, quickly shut his mouth. The vice president gave a derisive snort, then looked back to Monica. "I don't know what you did to butter up the prince, but I, for one, do not acknowledge you as a council member," he growled, opening the door.

Neil beckoned Monica inside, and she nervously followed after them.

Three people were already seated in the room. Felix, the president, sat at the desk in the middle. A droopy-eyed young man was at a separate conference table—Elliott, one of the secretaries. Also at the conference table was a beautiful girl with blond hair doing clerical work.

O-oh, she's... That intense beauty was unforgettable—it was the girl who had been playing the piano in the music room. *I guess she's a council member, too...*

The beautiful girl didn't even glance in Monica's direction; she simply kept her feather pen moving in silence. As Monica was wondering whether to say something, Felix spoke up, voice calm. "Looks like we're all here."

At that, everyone naturally gravitated toward the conference table—leaving open the seats at the head and foot of the table. The seat next to Neil, the foot, was probably Monica's. Felix gestured for her to take it, as he himself took his seat at the head.

"Now then. As I explained yesterday, I have appointed Lady Monica Norton as our new accountant to replace Aaron O'Brien. We'll do self-introductions; I'll start. I am Felix Arc Ridill, student council president."

Once Felix had given his name, the others had to follow suit. Cyril's face scrunched up bitterly as he spoke. "...I'm Cyril Ashley, the vice president."

The hostility in his voice was directed straight at Monica. She cowered as Elliott casually raised a hand.

"I already introduced myself yesterday, but I'm Elliott Howard, one of the secretaries."

At a glance, his attitude seemed approachable and familiar, but his droopy eyes were observing her coolly.

Once Elliott was done, the beautiful girl Monica had met in the music room the previous day took her turn. "I'm Bridget Greyham, the other secretary," she said flatly, not turning to look at Monica. Finished with her brief self-introduction, she put her folding fan up to her mouth and fell silent.

Finally, Neil made his introduction, a little embarrassed, from where he sat beside her. "I'm Neil Clay Maywood, officer of general affairs...even though I just introduced myself, ah-ha-ha." Neil's feigned laughter did nothing to loosen the tension in the room.

As if to improve the mood, Felix continued. "Then the last one is Lady Monica Norton. Please introduce yourself."

Oh, why did she keep having to introduce herself lately? She was so bad at it. She wanted to get up right now and run away. *But if I did that, Louis would scold me. Louis would scold me...and he's scary, really scary...*

She envisioned Louis Miller in her mind. *What's this, my fellow Sage? Can you not even say your own name properly? Ha-ha-ha. Your voice is like the cry of a cicada on the verge of death. Whenever did a cicada join the Sages? If you are too incompetent, they will think I am incompetent as well. If you understand, then straighten up and be a human, Cicada Girl.*

Just imagining it almost made her want to cry. She sniffled. Then, with a weak voice, she introduced herself.

"...I'm...M-Monica Norton..."

She'd said it. She'd said it! She'd stammered a little, but she had done much better than usual.

But someone at the table didn't seem to agree.

"How unsightly."

It was Bridget, the secretary. She set her amber eyes on Monica and, keeping her fan covering her mouth, continued. "I have never heard of a student council member who couldn't even say her name properly." As Monica's shoulders trembled, Bridget turned her cold stare to Felix. "Your Royal Highness, I question this girl's qualification to stand before others. I ask that you reconsider before it damages the reputation of this council."

As always, Felix's smile was gentle—his eyes narrowed somewhat, almost amused. "Does my selection not satisfy you?"

"It does not." Bridget nodded. She was firm, apparently seeing no need for fear or flattery toward the prince. "Are there not others here who think the same?"

Cyril was the first one to react. He stood from his seat, clenched his fist, and pleaded his case. "Sir, I am of the same opinion as Secretary Greyham. Please reconsider! To put someone at your side who has disrespected you is simply…"

Elliott watched Cyril's emphatic speech with amusement, while Neil seemed to be at a loss for what to do. Through it all, however, Felix's calm smile never faltered. But though his lips smiled, his blue eyes shone coldly.

"If Lady Norton has committed some sort of misconduct," said Felix, "then the responsibility for it falls upon me for appointing her. If that ever happens, you have my word that I will step down as student council president."

That remark shocked the other council members, but the most surprised of all was doubtlessly Monica.

Wa-wa-wa-wa-wa-wa-wa-wait! Wait, wait, wait! To be honest, she couldn't see herself *not* messing up. She would definitely mess up. She *knew* she would. Outside of numbers, she was hopeless. A failure—worse than mediocre.

As she sat there and started to shake, Felix lightly clapped his hands. "I think that about wraps it up. Cyril, I'd like you to show Lady Norton the ropes of the accounting job right away," he instructed.

Cyril opened his mouth to speak—dissatisfaction plain on his face. But he swallowed his objection down and reluctantly nodded. "…As you say, sir." As he raised his head, he leveled a glare at Monica. His eyes glistened with hostility.

Of all people, why is it him teaching me my job?! Trembling madly, Monica looked up at Felix. "E-e-e-excuse, excuse me... Why—why the vice president?"

"Cyril was the accountant before he assumed his current role." Felix paused, peering at Monica's face in what seemed like amusement. "Did you perhaps want me to teach you instead?"

"No, I was just, um, thinking maybe someone, um, closer in age..."

In other words, Neil—the one who seemed most pleasant and harmless.

"I see," said Felix, giving a gentle smile. "Cyril will keep you from slacking."

Monica whimpered.

* * *

"The beginning and end of the month are the busiest times for an accountant," said Cyril. "I've made a list of all your responsibilities, so you'd better memorize it."

Cyril Ashley's attitude toward Monica was blatantly aggressive, but he did a good job of explaining her tasks. She was curious about one thing, though—he'd placed a large glass on the table. Between parts of his explanation, he would chant a short incantation and drop one or two pieces of ice into the empty glass.

She was understandably curious about this, so once Cyril's description had reached a break, she nervously asked, "U-um... That ice... What do...you use it for?"

"It's for shoving into your mouth every time you make a mistake."

"Eep."

Cyril fiddled with his broach—maybe a nervous habit—and dropped another piece of ice into the vessel.

Suddenly, Monica noticed something. She could feel a chill from around Cyril—the kind of chill that came with ice mana. But the chill was suppressed while he created the ice pieces.

Wait... Could that be why he's doing it?

After finishing his explanation of the basics, Cyril shook the ice-filled glass a bit and snorted, sounding displeased. "Hmph. If you had been slow to learn, I would have jammed these right into your mouth...but it seems that won't be necessary."

Was that Cyril's version of a passing grade?

"If you have time to be distracted, spend it looking at the documents instead."

"Y-yes, sir, I'm sorry...!"

Flustered, Monica began skimming the papers. Her task itself wasn't actually very complicated. Before coming here, she'd worked with things like financial records, revenue and expenditure records, product sales changes, and population reports—if it had to do with numbers, she'd had a hand in it. Compared with all that, this wasn't much work.

As she read through the documents, she stole a glance at Cyril. During his explanation, he'd been collecting the old accounting records.

"Um, are those...the records that, um, I reviewed?" she asked nervously.

Cyril sniffed. "Yes. I'm getting them all together for Mr. Thornlee to review tonight. He agreed to look them over while he was on the night shift."

"I-I'm sorry!" apologized Monica reflexively.

He scowled at her, confused. "What are you apologizing for?"

"You h-have more, um, unnecessary work to do because, um, I reviewed...all the old records...don't you?"

The day before, Monica had been so thrilled to work with numbers again that she'd gone through every past document. Because of that, she now felt bad for giving Cyril and Mr. Thornlee more work.

Cyril glared at her. "This isn't unnecessary work. It's *quite* necessary. Why are you so timid all the time anyway?"

"U-um, um... I, well..."

"You've already won the prince's trust, you know. You can be proud of that. Why do you insist on being so overly humble?"

Those were words that Monica was used to hearing.

Why do you humble yourself so much?

You should be proud of your talents.

If you put yourself down, what are those even less skilled supposed to think?

Every person Monica knew had told her something like that. And their expressions made it clear they struggled to understand—just like Cyril now.

"The prince has *chosen* you. Acknowledged your talents. Why aren't you proud of it?"

Don't be overly modest. Don't put yourself down. Have confidence. You're talented... When she'd learned to use magecraft without chanting, she'd been told such things endlessly.

But Monica could never, ever nod and go along with it.

She wasn't rejecting those who *did* have pride in themselves—having pride in something was good. It was wonderful to be able to have confidence in your own talents. If that was something Monica could do, she would have done it.

But it wasn't, and she couldn't.

"I'm sorry...," she muttered, shaking her head slowly. "I just can't...can't have pride in myself...no matter what. I just...can't."

Back when she'd gone to Minerva's, there had been only one person she was able to call her friend. A young man who was always trying to help the shy Monica. He would practice chanting with her since she couldn't speak well in front of others. It had made Monica happy.

...But when she learned how to cast spells without chanting and began to be lauded as a genius, that friendship had broken apart.

You've been looking down on me this whole time, haven't you?

No, she had said. *No*—but her words hadn't reached him.

Monica had graduated from Minerva's and become one of the Seven Sages without ever making up with him. Even now, it remained a bitter memory, a lump in her heart.

As she hung her head, Cyril's face tightened into a scowl, and his lips turned down in displeasure. "I hate the word *can't*."

"…I'm sorry." Monica could only look down and apologize in response to Cyril's denunciation.

Someone once said talent could be a curse. That was the case for Monica. It took everything she wanted away from her—both her father and her friend.

"…Oh, and as for another matter," remarked Cyril casually as Monica tensed up, afraid of what might come next.

"This is about how you fell from the landing on the stairs yesterday."

"…Ah, that's, um…"

Caroline and Lana had gotten into an argument, and Caroline had pushed Lana into Monica. But Monica had thought the matter was resolved after she claimed to have fallen accidentally. Perhaps Cyril intended to scold her for her carelessness. She shuddered.

Cyril's expression turned severe. "I questioned students who had been nearby at the time, and I got a grasp on the situation. I've ordered Caroline Simmons, the assailant, to submit a letter of apology and gave her a stern warning."

"…Huh?"

Monica's eyes went wide—she didn't understand what Cyril was talking about. Caroline was the noble daughter of an elite family. That was why she'd been so confident at the time. She knew her social status made her impervious to criticism. If Monica tried to accuse Caroline, Lana would end up taking the blame. That was why Monica had given up on telling the truth and had instead attempted to resolve the situation by saying the fall was her own fault.

"…You questioned…them?"

"How else would I get an accurate and objective understanding of the situation?" Cyril was acting like she'd just asked him what two plus two was. "Anyway, you need to give a truthful and accurate account next time something like that happens! Your poor attempt at a lie made more work for me! No more false reports!"

Monica's mouth hung open as she blankly stared at Cyril. She hadn't thought anyone would listen to her, no matter what she'd said. That was why she'd given up right away and stayed silent.

So people like this do *exist...* Surprised and refreshed, she looked up at Cyril.

He raised his eyebrows as he continued to glare at her. "Are you listening to me, Monica Norton?!"

"Oh, um, yes... I, w-well..." As she twiddled her thumbs and tried to stammer out the next words, someone tapped Monica on the shoulder.

"How are things going here?"

She looked back to see Felix smiling pleasantly at her.

Cyril answered immediately and succinctly. "I've explained all the usual tasks, including those at the beginning and end of the month. All that remains is to explain school events."

"Ah yes. We do have the chess tournament and the school festival before winter break. You can explain those to her gradually."

"Yes, sir." Cyril nodded.

Felix glanced at the glass on the desk and casually picked it up. The ice pieces clunked against one another. After a moment, he said, "Are you not feeling well, Cyril?"

"No problems here, sir."

"Oh? Well, that's fine... Don't overdo it, though."

What were they talking about?

When Lord Ashley creates ice, does that mean he's not feeling well? she mused. The chill he naturally emanated, the ice he'd gone to the trouble of creating and dropping in the glass, the broach he toyed with like a nervous habit...

Actually, Monica had an idea that made sense of all of it. *Wait, could he...?*

As she gazed at Cyril's broach, fingers reached in from the side and poked her in the face. She looked over; Felix was squishing her cheek, apparently enjoying himself. "Don't look just at Cyril. Look at me, too."

"I... I-I-I'm so-sor..."

"How *dare* you! Your attitude besmirches His Royal Highness's honor!"

"I'm s-s-s-sorr…," stammered Monica, half crying.

Cyril pounded the desk with a fist. "Speak clearly!"

"I! I'm! I'm—I'm…sorr…"

"I don't remember asking you to add staccato!"

"Cyril, please don't bully her too much, all right?" chided Felix as Cyril shouted angrily.

The latter's face sharpened. "I am not bullying her, sir! This is discipline!"

"Discipline is the pet owner's job, right? Which means it's *my* job."

Monica felt like he'd just casually stripped her of her human rights. For now, she decided to escape from reality by counting the number of Felix's eyelashes.

CHAPTER 9

A Midnight Visitor and a Happy Feller

After finishing dinner in the dormitory, Monica returned to her attic room and sat down on her bed.

"I'm so tired...but I should change..."

Sluggishly, she got back up to her feet, removed her uniform, and smoothed out the wrinkles before hanging it up. Then she put on her hooded robe. While she was at it, maybe she'd let down her hair as well and put it into a loose pair of hanging braids.

She reached for the ribbon. But she ended up leaving it, instead moving her fingers across the hair Lana had so neatly styled for her.

Her classmates looked at her differently now that she was a student council member. Most of their gazes were jealous or suspicious, wondering how and why a girl like her had been selected. But Lana didn't hate her. She'd talked to Monica the same way she always did.

...And that alone was enough to make Monica very happy.

It would be a waste to undo it, she thought, figuring she could wear it like this until it was time to bathe. She left it as it was and fell onto her bed face-first.

A moment later, there was a clattering at the window—Nero. After coming into the room, he politely used his front paw to close the window behind him.

"Good work today, Monica."

He jumped onto Monica's back as she lay facedown on the bed and pressed his front paws onto her shoulder blades. The pressure was a little weak for a massage, but the squish of his soft paws felt good. Absorbed in the sensation, Monica closed her eyes and breathed a sigh.

"How did your first day at student council go?" he asked.

"…Lord Ashley…made sure I didn't slack off…"

"Ashley? Oh, I remember now. That chilly guy who's always near the prince, yelling at everyone, right? Who never stops leaking ice mana? I know all about the prince *and* everyone around him! Amazing, right?"

"…But not their names, huh?"

"I'm awful at remembering human names. So anyway, he worked you pretty hard? Was it worse than Lou-lou-lou Lounpappa?"

Evidently, Nero had no intention of learning either Cyril's name *or* Louis's. Monica grinned wryly and answered, "Hmm… I would say Lord Ashley is about… one–one hundredth as strict as Mr. Louis."

"What is that guy, a demon?"

Cyril's speaking style was harsh and exhausting, but his instruction had been cordial. He'd made a list of everything she'd need, and when she didn't understand something, he took the time to explain it. *Compared with him, Louis is…* She remembered those nightmarish days under his instruction and instantly deflated. But then she heard a knocking sound from the window.

She craned her neck to look at it and saw a bird perched on the sill. It was a beautiful, small bird with yellow and yellow-green plumage. Was it an ornamental pet that had run away from its noble master?

The bird continued to peck at the window with its beak and showed no signs of fear when Nero approached. On a hunch, Monica opened the window. The bird flew into the room, made a circuit around it, then landed on the floor. Eventually, small particles of light appeared around the bird, and it morphed into a woman wearing a maid's outfit.

"You're, um, Louis's…"

The maid pinched the hem of her skirt, curtseyed. Then, in a monotone voice, she said, "It is I, Rynzbelfeid, contracted spirit of the Barrier Mage Louis Miller. Please call me Ryn."

Monica unconsciously straightened her back—they'd just been speaking about Louis being a demon, after all.

Louis had probably sent Ryn, his contracted spirit, to get a report on how the mission was progressing.

"Um, er, you…you want a report on the, um, mission, right?"

"Yes, but first, I have a pressing message to deliver from Lord Louis."

A pressing message? That meant it was something she needed to hear right away. *What could it be?* thought Monica and Nero with bated breath.

Ryn opened her mouth, face still impassive. "I, Louis Miller, am about to…"

"A-about to…?" repeated Monica.

"…become a dad."

Monica was at a loss for words.

"Who caaares!" yelled Nero. "Why is that important?! It's just a personal message!"

Nero began punching the floor with his front paw, but Ryn seemed unfazed.

"Yes," she continued. "The mistress is now pregnant, and Lord Louis is quite the happy feller."

"…F-feller?" repeated Monica. She hadn't heard that term before.

"Yes. A happy feller," repeated Ryn, face serious. "Apparently, in western areas of the kingdom, *feller* is another word for *man*. As such, a *happy feller* is a man brimming with cheer."

"I, um, I see…"

"I have been wanting to use it ever since I saw it in a book. I'm quite moved to have finally gotten the chance."

She claimed to be moved, but her face was still as impassive as always. Monica could never tell if she was joking.

"Um... Well... Please tell Mr. Louis and his wife, um, congratulations."

"This is your chance to get angry, Monica! That wicked mage forced you to do this difficult mission, and now he's enjoying himself! Get as angry as you want!" cried Nero, raising his paws to emphasize his point.

But Monica honestly wished them well. Louis aside, his wife, Rosalie, had taken very good care of Monica during her stay with them.

"I shall inform them." Ryn nodded, producing a sheet of paper from somewhere on her person. "Now that the main issue is taken care of, I—"

"Wait! That was the main issue?!" exclaimed Nero.

Ryn ignored him and unfolded the paper on the desk. On it was a message scrawled in Louis's handwriting.

"Dear Silent Witch. I am well aware of your incompetence regarding giving oral reports. Please record any important information on this paper and give it back to Ryn."

Her fellow Sage knew her well. If she'd had to give her report orally, she'd have missed half the important details.

"I will be your messenger pigeon for the duration of this mission. If you have any reports or messages for Lord Louis, please write them down and give them to me. I will ensure that they are delivered at once."

"...U-um, what if there's no particular news to report?"

"Then I will remain here until there is."

"I-I'll start right away!"

Flustered, Monica moved her lamp to the desk. Fortunately, she had quite a bit to report—about how she'd resolved the flowerpot incident and been appointed to the student council. These were both important developments for her mission, so she could probably include them with pride.

Oh, and this... And that... More and more came to mind.

As she was thinking about what to write, Nero's whiskers twitched, and he turned toward the window.

"Hey, Monica," he said, "there's something chilly behind the boys' dorm."

"...Huh?"

Monica was confused, not understanding what he was getting at. Then Ryn jumped in. "I am reading ice mana behind the boys' dormitory. It seems to be an uncontrolled outpouring of mana rather than a conscious usage of magecraft."

Monica had a bad feeling about this. A chill ran down her spine. The words *ice mana* made her immediately think of the council's vice president, Cyril Ashley.

"...Um, Ryn, you said the reading is coming from outside the dorm, right? Not inside?"

"Yes, it's coming from the outside and slowly moving away from the dormitories."

If the reading was coming from Cyril, did that mean a serious student like him had snuck out of the dorm this late at night? Either way, as the second prince's bodyguard, she couldn't overlook any unusual incidents near the boys' dorm.

"I'll... I'll go have a look..."

"Wait up, Monica. How are you planning to get out of the girls' dorm? You can't use flight magecraft, can you?"

"Ack!"

Nero was right. Flight magecraft required a good sense of balance in addition to excellent mana control, making it very difficult for Monica, who had disastrous motor skills. Experienced veterans could freely fly through the sky, but she could only jump a little higher in the air at most.

As Monica stared uneasily down from the window, Ryn made a modest suggestion.

"In that case, you may leave it to me. As a wind spirit, flight magecraft is my specialty."

Come to think of it, Ryn had also been the one to carry her from her mountain cabin to the royal capital. *She's so dependable!* thought Monica, looking up at Ryn with admiration.

With one foot already on the window frame, Ryn said, "Regarding the landing method, I have recently devised something new called a *hurricane landing.* I highly recommend it, as it presents a chance to experience the wonders of centrifugal force with your entire body."

"Th-that's, um… You're…joking, right?" asked Monica cautiously.

"……"

Ryn looked at her without saying a word. Her eyes, the color of fresh grass, were unclouded. They were so clear, in fact, that Monica was a little frightened.

Snatching up Nero and holding him to her chest, she cried, "Please just make it safe!"

* * *

Felix was sitting in his dorm room drinking black tea. His spirit, Wildianu, was currently in the form of a white lizard. He poked his head out of Felix's pocket and said, "Sir?"

Felix replaced his cup on the saucer, then let Wildianu climb up on his fingertips.

"…Is it Cyril?"

"Yes. I feel powerful ice mana outside the dorm."

"Can you pinpoint it?"

"…I apologize, sir. I can only give you a general direction."

Wildianu sounded contrite, but this was something they couldn't do anything about. His forte as a water spirit was illusion and distraction, and his detection abilities were limited.

"What shall we do, then? I can't very well leave him be… Perhaps I'll go take a look."

Felix rose, donning the jacket that had been hanging over the back of his chair.

* * *

My head... It hurts...

Outside the boys' dormitory, the figure of a young man could be seen walking, his gait unsteady. He was slender, wore the uniform of Serendia Academy, and sported long silver hair that shone in the moonlight—it was the student council vice president, Cyril Ashley.

His fair cheeks were slick with an unhealthy sweat. Scrunching up his face in pain, he headed away from the dormitory and entered the adjacent forest.

"...Urgh, ah..."

Throb. Each time the sharp pain ran through his head, the mana in his body surged out of control. Cyril quickly said a chant and put his hand on a nearby tree. Instantly, the tree was covered in ice.

Cyril Ashley had a condition known as mana hyperabsorption.

Humans possess a vessel for storing mana. When that mana depletes, such as through the use of magecraft, the vessel slowly refills itself by absorbing mana from outside the body. However, humans are not able to store more mana than the vessel can hold. Once it is full, the body rejects any further mana, ceasing to absorb it.

But that was not the case for Cyril. Even after his vessel had filled, his body still believed more mana was required and continued to absorb it. This condition was referred to as mana hyperabsorption. An excess of mana could damage the body and lead to mana poisoning; therefore, every once in a while, he would have to release it.

Groaning, Cyril clutched the broach at his neck, which secured his tie. The broach was actually a magical item that forcibly expelled the excess mana in his body. With its help, he should be able to go about his daily life without issue. But ever since the previous day, he had been feeling unwell.

If he used magecraft, the amount of mana in his body would decrease. That would make it easier for a time, but soon his body would start absorbing more.

The absorption also appeared to be taking place much faster than usual. Too fast. No matter how many spells he cast, he couldn't seem to run out of mana. In fact, it seemed like he was absorbing it faster than he could use it up.

He dropped to his knees, curled in on himself, and grasped his magical broach like a lifeline. Marquess Highown had given this to him—it was his treasure.

Cyril wasn't originally from the marquess's family. Because Marquess Highown had only been blessed with a daughter, he had selected Cyril as the most talented of his distant relatives and adopted him.

Though Cyril's family technically shared Marquess Highown's bloodline, they didn't even have a noble rank—they were at the bottom of the bottom. Cyril had been chosen anyway. There could be only one reason: his talent.

Cyril, who had been cooped up in his town, attending the local school, had been proud to be chosen for his talent. He'd entered Lord Ashley's house full of pride and joy, and what he had found when he arrived was the marquess's daughter, his younger stepsister.

House Highown was called the Lineage of the Wise. His new little sister was possessed of vast intelligence, as befitting such a nickname. She was far, far more talented than Cyril.

Why, then, had he become the marquess's foster child?

On the verge of losing his sense of purpose, he desperately immersed himself in every field of study there was. But no matter how much he did, he could never close the gap with her. In fact, the more he learned, the more he realized how wide a gap it was.

Deciding instead to devise a weapon of his own, he'd studied magecraft—only to be brought low by his reckless practice and the mana hyperabsorption sickness it had given him.

The more he struggled, the further he drifted from his ideal. It made him feel hopeless—and that was when his foster father, Marquess Highown, had given him this magic broach.

Keeping this on him would suppress his mana hyperabsorption—that was what the marquess had told him when he had gifted him the broach. To Cyril, it had felt like the marquess was accepting him, recognizing his place in the family. He had been overjoyed. He wanted to meet the marquess's expectations. And more than anything else...

I want......to believe in me.

Cyril didn't have time to be crawling about like this. But despite his wishes, his body kept absorbing mana. He quickly chanted and unleashed an ice spell. The ground before him froze over, but as soon as he felt the slight physical relief, his body started absorbing mana again.

His mana absorption rate had changed at times when he was unhealthy, but this pace was abnormal.

Why? Why? Why...?! I need to chant again to use another spell, he thought before his head throbbed again.

His pulse started fluctuating, and his breathing grew ragged. He couldn't chant like this. He couldn't use magecraft.

"Ah...guh..."

Cyril clawed at the ground with his hands, his body convulsing and covered in a cold sweat.

Eventually, everything went dark, and his consciousness began to fade.

But before he completely blacked out, he heard a cat's meow.

* * *

With the help of Ryn's flight magic, she, Monica, and Nero had escaped Monica's dorm room. From there, they had followed Cyril's trail of mana into the forest, where they found him under a tree. He was writhing in pain, firing off ice spells at random. Clearly, he was not well.

Ryn tilted her head in a gesture of confusion, though her face was still impassive.

"I hadn't realized students these days secretly practiced mage-craft in the middle of the night. How diligent."

"No, um… I think Lord Ashley is experiencing mana poisoning, um, from mana hyperabsorption illness."

"Mana poisoning?" Ryn and Nero repeated together. Neither of them seemed familiar with the concept.

"W-well, a human body has low mana resistance compared to spirits or dragons, so if they absorb too much, they become unwell… It's called mana poisoning… At worst, it can result in death."

Monica had seen several people with the same symptoms before, when she'd been going to Minerva's Mage Training Institution. Mana hyperabsorption was divided into five stages based on the severity, and Cyril's symptoms seemed to indicate he was at the highest of those.

"Someone like Lord Ashley, who naturally absorbs mana easily, probably uses magecraft frequently to decrease his store of mana, or he wears a magic item that absorbs the excess for him…"

That would explain why Cyril regularly converted mana into chilly air and released it and why he'd been filling that glass with pieces of ice. That was how he expelled excess mana from his system. The fact that he kept fiddling with the broach at his neck likely meant it was a magic item for absorbing mana.

After hearing Monica's explanation, Ryn made a loop with her thumb and index finger, then peered through it at Cyril. "I can see the flow of mana. His broach is collecting the mana expelled from his body and then returning it."

"I knew it…! The magic item is malfunctioning…!"

The item was doing the opposite of what it was supposed to do. They had to get the broach off him as soon as possible.

But if Monica drew near, he'd probably demand to know what she was doing here. She had the hood of her robe up, but that wouldn't be enough to fool him if she got close enough to touch the broach.

As she hesitated, Nero gave a heroic-sounding meow. "Just leave it to me!"

Nero sprang out from the trees and jumped on Cyril, grabbing the broach at the boy's neck with his mouth.

"What? A cat...?! Stop... Don't touch that!"

Cyril swung his arms around, trying to resist, but Nero easily evaded them and removed the broach before jumping away.

"Give it... Give it back!" screamed Cyril hysterically, eyes blood-shot, before he began to quickly chant a spell.

A moment later, a wall of ice was blocking Nero's path.

Urgh?! Flustered, Nero changed direction and tried to flee into the forest...but the wall of ice rapidly expanded to block that way, too. The next thing he knew, the wall had surrounded him and Cyril.

Oh, damn... And I haaate the cold!

"Give it back... Give that back..." Cyril closed in on Nero, eyes bloodshot. Nero could hear hollow groans between his ragged breaths. "That's... My father...gave it...to me... Need him to...accept...acknowledge me..." His eyes were clouded with obsession and had lost the light of sanity.

Nero couldn't help but pity the boy. *Why are humans all such total morons?* he thought. He knew this human probably had his own reasons for being so attached to the broach. But those reasons didn't have anything to do with Nero.

Cyril quickly chanted a spell. More than a dozen ice arrows appeared in the air around him, floating. Each one was the thickness of a person's arm—they were more like stakes than arrows. Either way, getting hit by one of those was going to hurt. A lot.

"He acknowledged me. My stepfather...the prince, too...so then, why...?" Cyril's fevered, hollow gaze was fixed on Nero. But it wasn't Nero he saw. Instead, as the mana ravaged his body, he was hallucinating someone else, someone Nero didn't know and couldn't see.

"…Why…?"

His handsome features twisted in pain and what looked like sadness. "Why…won't you acknowledge me…Mother…?"

Suddenly, the wall of ice collapsed without a sound. That, along with the ice arrows floating around him, went up in flames and burned. The ice he'd produced melted within seconds, and the flames that had melted it, as if possessed of a will, coalesced into one spot until they transformed into a great, fiery serpent.

On the other side of the collapsed ice wall stood a small witch, hood pulled low over her eyes, standing with the white moon at her back.

This was the master of unchanted magecraft and one of the Seven Sages—Monica Everett, the Silent Witch.

* * *

Though the blood of House Highown had run through Cyril's father's veins, he hadn't possessed a noble rank, and their family was far from affluent. But his father was full of pride over his noble connection, refusing to find proper work and behaving high-handedly toward Cyril's mother.

Cyril had hated it and had always sided with his mother. He'd done what he could to try and make her happy. But whenever his mother looked at him—at his noble face that so closely resembled his father's—she would always frown in sadness and avert her eyes.

Eventually, his father had drowned himself in alcohol and died. It was around that time that someone from House Highown had come to speak with Cyril about his potential adoption.

Cyril had jumped for joy. He could make things easier for his mother! He could make her happy!

Seeing her son's innocent happiness, his mother had heaved a sigh and said, "You really are a noble, just as I'd thought."

No. Mother, I'm your son.

But he couldn't say those words, no matter how hard he tried.

*   *   *

In front of Cyril stood a hooded figure. The figure was small; he couldn't imagine it was an adult. But when the person lifted their right arm, the flaming serpent that had melted his ice wall coiled around them.

The black cat that had stolen Cyril's broach gave a meow before running over to the hooded figure. The person picked up the cat, then plucked the broach out of his mouth.

"...Does that cat belong to you?" growled Cyril.

The hooded figure didn't look at him, however. They were focused on the broach.

Their attitude was making Cyril more and more irritated. "Give me back that broach!" he exclaimed, chanting a spell in his rage— one to create chains of ice.

When Cyril snapped his fingers, his ice chains would wrap themselves tight around the hooded figure's limbs...but a moment later, his chains fell to pieces.

"...Huh?"

The hooded figure hadn't done anything. They hadn't even chanted. And yet, the ice chains had shattered like brittle glass, their fragments glistening and scattering across the ground.

Thinking he'd made a mistake with the formula, Cyril chanted the spell a second time. But the result was no different—they collapsed as soon as they materialized.

"Why, why...? You... Is this your doing?"

The hooded figure remained silent and stared at the broach, as though Cyril wasn't even worth a look.

...It was eerie.

"Answer me!" he demanded, creating arrows of ice and shooting them at the hooded figure.

But right before they connected, they were engulfed in flames and melted away. Cyril assumed the person had a friend nearby. He couldn't explain it otherwise. After all, the hooded figure had never chanted anything. And there was no way they could have nullified Cyril's spells without doing so.

"Damn it… Damn it…!"

He created a lot more ice arrows this time, then fired them in random directions. If the hooded figure had an accomplice, he wanted to smoke them out. But the figure casually raised a hand—and with just that, the ice arrows burst into flame and melted away like they'd never existed.

What…? What is that…?

It wasn't that difficult to use a shield to block randomly fired arrows. But to shoot every single one of them down? The level of technique required was unimaginable. The magecraft Cyril had just witnessed, however, had done exactly that. What's more, once the flames had melted the ice, they had disappeared without burning the nearby trees. That was a clear indication of how exact the magecraft had been. Each one of the flames had been constructed with terrifyingly precise calculations. And that many? Within seconds?

What…what—what is even happening? What am I seeing?

Someone unfamiliar with magecraft would have been distracted by the giant flaming serpent, since it had such a flashy appearance. But anyone who had even so much as tried their hand at a spell would have known how unusual those tiny flames that had melted the ice arrows had been.

Shields were the fundamental defense in mage combat—in other words, defensive barriers. But the person in front of him hadn't used a shield at all, suggesting an overwhelming difference in technique between them and Cyril.

"What…what *are* you…?" Cyril abandoned the idea of delicate control. He converted all the mana he could into ice-cold air and rammed it into the hooded figure. "Freeze! Freeze, damn you! I'll turn you into a silent ice sculpture!" he wailed hysterically.

The cold wave with Cyril at its center began to freeze everything in sight. The ground, the trees—and even Cyril himself. What did he care about frostbite on his limbs? He continued at full force.

Then, however, he noticed it. The cold wave he had created with all his power was being pushed back—no, it was being diverted, straight up into the air.

The hooded figure was redirecting Cyril's cold wave with wind magecraft.

Simultaneously, the frost stuck to Cyril's limbs began to flake off and fall to the ground. A barrier had been cast on his body to protect him from the cold. Cyril had used this spell without concern for himself—it wasn't him creating the barrier.

Then are they *doing it...?*

If the hooded figure was using a wind spell to redirect his cold wave, and a defensive barrier was protecting him physically... In other words, they were likely using two advanced spells *at the same time.*

The hooded figure's accomplice was probably hiding somewhere nearby, quietly chanting their spells. That had to be it.

But...what if that wasn't the case?

If that hooded figure was using this much magecraft by themselves...then they had to be some kind of monster.

The color drained from Cyril's face, and he began to tremble. The feeling of excitement and intoxication that had come with using his spells had faded, and his skin grew pale.

"Ah..." His vision hazed over, and his body went completely limp. He'd reached the end of his mana. "No such thing as *can't*...I...I'm..."

Cyril gritted his teeth, trying to retain consciousness. But it was no use. His body became heavy, and his vision darkened.

"I...I need to...live up to..."

Right before passing out, Cyril saw something—the hooded figure running toward him, hopelessly clumsy, before extending a small hand.

* * *

"A-a-a-are you...are you all right...?!" exclaimed Monica as she ran over to Cyril. She set his head on her lap and began to examine him.

He was unconscious, and his pulse was a bit weak, but he would survive. A little rest and he'd be back on his feet.

"…Thank goodness."

In its early stages, mana poisoning gave one a strong sense of excitement when using magecraft. At later stages, it could cause hallucinations, heart palpitations, and dizziness, and at worst, the mana would eat away at a person's body until they died. The fastest way to cure someone's mana poisoning was to have them use magecraft until their mana ran out while still in the early stages of illness.

"Excellent job."

Ryn appeared—she'd been watching from the shadows—and looked at the broach in Monica's hands. "Is the item malfunctioning, as you expected?"

"Yes… A flaw has appeared in the formula… I don't think it had a protection formula on it."

Magical items were extremely sensitive. They were, quite literally, items that guided the flow of mana. If the mana wasn't being guided by a correct formula, then it would likely malfunction. Therefore, generally, one would overlay a protection formula in order to protect it.

However, Cyril's broach had no such measure.

"Magic items without a protection formula frequently malfunction when the bearer receives a strong magical attack."

"So it's a defective product?!" cried Nero, waving his tail in irritation. "Geez! So who was cutting corners?"

"Um… There's a maker's mark engraved on the back of it…"

Monica flipped over the broach and read the name. Her expression soured. "…Emanuel Darwin, the Gem Mage."

"Who's that? Huh? Anyone know him?"

As Monica struggled to answer, Ryn cut in, her tone matter-of-fact.

"He, like the Silent Witch, is recorded as one of the Seven Sages. Not a friend of Lord Louis. Part of the second prince's faction. According to Lord Louis, he is a 'money-grubber.'"

After a few seconds of silence, Nero spoke up.

"Do any of the Seven Sages have their head on straight?"

The remark struck home. Monica put a hand to her chest and groaned before overwriting the broach with a new magical formula.

This sort of spell, which bestowed mana upon matter, was called imbuement magecraft. Monica hadn't done any focused study on this subject, but the formula on this broach wasn't very complex in its construction, so she had an easy time revising it.

In contrast, the broach Louis had made for Felix was an extremely advanced magical item—not only did it track the bearer's whereabouts, it would also detect danger and create a defensive barrier if the wearer was to come under attack.

On the other hand, this broach was made only for absorbing and emitting mana.

Maybe I'll add in a self-regulating formula to control how much mana is absorbed based on how much he has in his body at any given time.

Whenever Monica saw magical formulas like this, she got the urge to improve them. It was a bad habit. Still, if the broach's functions changed significantly out of nowhere, Cyril would be confused. So Monica corrected the flaw in the magical formula, embedded a self-regulation formula, and stopped there. Then she overlaid two protective formulas. That should prevent future mishaps.

As she put the broach back on Cyril's collar, Nero looked up at her mischievously.

"Why do all that for nothing, hmm? You could wring a couple of gold coins out of him just for repairing it, right?"

"…Well, that's…"

Monica paused to get her words in order. She couldn't help but be a little bit jealous of Cyril. He was so proud of the fact that someone else had acknowledged him—and he worked diligently to gain that acknowledgment, sparing no effort.

"Having mana hyperabsorption comes with various issues, but if you learn to control it, a mage can turn it to their advantage."

If a person's rate of mana absorption was high, that also meant they could restore mana quickly. And faster recovery could grant an advantage over other mages during prolonged battles.

Actually, there were even mages who tried to induce it by purposely putting themselves through grueling training to try and raise their mana regeneration rate.

In other words, this condition of Cyril's had could easily be considered a talent.

"…I didn't want…him to see his talent as a curse."

Monica was never able to take pride in her own abilities. She couldn't help but think of them as a curse. But she didn't want Cyril to end up like her. She wanted him to be able to puff out his chest and be confident. To have enough pride to make up for Monica's lack of it.

"Hey, uh, by the way," said Nero, poking Cyril's cheek with his front paw. "Now what? Leave him here to sleep it off?"

He had raised a good point. Though it wasn't yet winter, Monica hesitated to leave someone in his condition out sleeping in the forest.

As she was wondering what to do, Ryn raised her hand. "I can use a gust of wind to blow his body back into the boys' dormitory."

"I'd rather do something a little less violent…"

"Then I'll engulf him in a tornado and send him flying back to the dorm—"

"That sounds even worse!"

Still, even if Ryn was to sneak into the boys' dorm using flight magic, she wouldn't be able to find Cyril's room. Monica was at a loss.

At last, Nero gave a dramatic sigh and leaped into the air. He did a flip before landing, and a moment later, he was a black cat no more. In his place stood a young man with black hair and golden eyes.

"I'll go carry him to the gate of the boys' dorm. If I leave him lying on the ground close by, someone's bound to notice, right?"

Monica groaned. "Do you really have to leave him lying there?"

"Wouldn't make sense for me to sneak inside and get us both

caught, would it?" said Nero, roughly lifting Cyril's body and throwing him over his shoulder.

"Um, Nero, can you at least put him on your back...?"

Nero ignored her and lightly kicked off the ground into a sprint. Eventually, his silhouette melted into the dark forest.

CHAPTER 10
The Perfect Formula

With Cyril over his shoulder, Nero dashed through the pitch-black forest. Even in human form, he had improved night vision. In addition, he was much stronger than the average human and could easily maintain his full speed despite carrying Cyril.

...Come to think of it, he thought, *how did this chilly guy sneak out of the dorm?*

The boys' and girls' dormitories were each surrounded by high walls. Guards manned the gates, keeping watch throughout the night. It should have been quite difficult to get in or out.

If one could use flight magic to soar or leap through the air, that would be a different story, but flight magic wasn't as easy as it sounded. It required both a high level of precision mana control and developed physical abilities—it was a technique primarily used by high mages. That was why Monica, with her below-average physical coordination, couldn't use it.

In my expert opinion, this chilly guy has some standout ice magecraft, but he doesn't seem to be particularly skilled at anything else.

A person's elemental affinity was determined from birth, and most average mages were only able to manipulate a single element. Monica's ability to easily handle advanced magecraft without regard to element was in many ways unusual. Though Nero found it easy to forget at times, she *was* one of the Seven Sages—the greatest mages in the kingdom—after all.

Chilly guy probably can't use wind spells, then. Though it's still pretty amazing that he can use ice magecraft so well at his age. How had Cyril, who couldn't use flight magic, snuck out of the boys' dorm?

The answer came to him the moment he arrived at the rear entrance to the dormitory. There was a large crack in part of the wall surrounding the building. Cyril must have slipped through it.

"For an elite academy," muttered Nero, "that's sure some sloppy maintenance work."

"Apparently, generations of students have used that crack to slip out of the dorm and take a breather," came a voice from behind Nero.

He turned back, Cyril still over his shoulder, and saw a familiar male student standing behind him. With a tall, slender body; a pleasantly handsome face; and golden hair that shone softly in the moonlight—it was the second prince of the Kingdom of Ridill, Felix Arc Ridill. He was wearing his school uniform and holding a rather large board.

As Nero looked at the board, Felix stood it up against the wall so as to cover the crack. "Normally we conceal it with the board like this, but it would seem Cyril wasn't able to do so at the time."

Ah, thought Nero. *So the prince is also a regular customer, too.* Nodding to himself, Nero lowered Cyril from his shoulder. "I'm a traveler who just happened to pass by. This chilly guy was out of control with mana poisoning and collapsed in the middle of the forest, so I brought him back here for you. What do you think? I'm so kind, right? Hurry up and thank me."

"Yes. Thank you for your efforts."

"Whatever he says he saw, tell him it was all a hallucination due to the mana poisoning. Got that? Everything he saw was a hallucination."

"…Hmm?" Felix glanced at Cyril, then immediately returned his gaze to Nero. His expression was calm and gentle—but his blue eyes were guarded as they watched Nero's movements. "Would you mind giving me your name, perhaps, kind traveler?"

"Oh, I'm no one important. But since I'm so nice, I'll tell you anyway. The name's Bartholomew Alexander."

Faced with Nero's braggadocio, Felix put a hand to his mouth and snickered.

"That's the same name as the main character in an adventure novel."

"Wait. You know Dustin Gunther?" Nero asked, excitement in his voice.

He felt his fondness for the prince increasing slightly. It was his firm belief that anyone who liked Dustin Gunther had to be a good person.

Felix shrugged. "I've partaken in most amusements this country has to offer—novels, games, theater," he said, smiling—though his smile seemed somehow empty.

Nero unconsciously scowled. *This guy gives me the creeps.*

Despite having been born into royalty and blessed with everything he could ever desire, the prince had empty eyes—like those of someone who possessed nothing at all.

Felix easily scooped up Cyril, then turned back to Nero as if he had just remembered something. "By the way, traveler? These forests are academy property, so only academy personnel and students are allowed to enter them."

"Oh. Is that right?"

Nero *hated* being told to follow human rules. *I'm not human, after all.* The rules of mankind were none of his concern. He gestured to Cyril with his chin. "Since I saved the chilly guy for you, just pretend you didn't see me."

"Yes, of course. I'm not about to interrogate you after you saved Cyril."

"Ohhh?" Nero knitted his brows in suspicion and shoved his hand into the folds of his robe. After rummaging around in the cloth, he appeared to catch something. "...Or maybe you didn't need to interrogate me because you were going to have your little spy check up on me instead," he said, bringing his hand back out of his robe.

Clutched between his fingers was the tail of a white lizard, his body swaying limply to and fro. Nero raised the lizard up to his face.

"Looks tasty!" he threatened.

The lizard flailed his tiny limbs.

Nero bared his sharp teeth in a villainous grin. "A water spirit, by the looks of it? You probably planned to have him hide in my clothes and keep tabs on me. Well, that's too bad for you. I'm pretty sensitive to mana."

Spirits were like big clumps of mana. The higher level the spirit, the harder it was for Nero to miss. This white lizard was a high water spirit, presumably contracted with the prince. Even presented with the white lizard, however, Felix maintained his calm smile—and that just made him even creepier.

Nero had been hoping for a bigger reaction, like, *Wh-what?!* or *Who in the world are you?!* Unfortunately, the prince showed no sign of agitation whatsoever.

Bored, Nero tossed the lizard to the ground and turned his back on Felix.

"See you."

Before leaving, Nero cocked his head a little and took one last look behind him. Felix said nothing—just stood there smiling quietly, watching him leave.

Look, you sparkly prince, he said to himself. *I don't care how bored you are. You keep your hands off my favorite, got it?*

He didn't want to give away his identity by continuing to chat, so he kept his mouth shut—but bared his sharp teeth in another villainous grin.

If you break Monica, I'll rip you to shreds and devour you.

After being tossed to the ground, Wildianu moved over to Felix and pressed his little head to the dirt in apology. "I'm terribly sorry for my lack of strength, sir. I shall begin pursuit of him right away and—"

"No, don't worry about it. We wouldn't want you getting eaten."

Though Felix spoke in a lighthearted, jovial way, Wildianu seemed to be very seriously ashamed of his incompetence.

At any rate, Felix had already given up on chasing the black-haired man. He didn't know who he was, but he felt instinctively that simply chasing the man down wouldn't be enough.

He wasn't human, whoever he was. He probably wasn't a spirit, either, but something else entirely. But regardless of his identity, if he didn't mean any harm to Felix, then Felix was more than happy to leave the matter be for now.

"Wil, return to my pocket. It would be inconvenient if Cyril was to see you."

"Of course, sir." Wildianu slithered up Felix's leg and tucked himself into the prince's pocket. Once he'd finished, Felix adjusted Cyril's position on his back and started walking.

He heard Cyril give a little groan. Apparently, he'd come to.

"Ugh... I, I...," he murmured, voice ragged.

Felix spoke to him in his usual tone. "Hey. Awake now?"

"...Prince...?" Cyril blinked several times, then looked at Felix, eyes hazy.

"You had a case of mana poisoning and collapsed in the forest. A kind traveler brought you back here."

"...I've caused you trouble."

"Oh, I don't mind."

Normally, Cyril would have suggested straightaway that he be allowed to walk on his own. The fact that he hadn't protested proved how exhausted he was.

Once Felix had delivered him to his room, Cyril wearily lay down on the bed and looked up at Felix. "...The traveler who rescued me. Was it a short person wearing a hood?"

Felix shook his head. "No, it was a tall man with black hair."

"...I see," murmured Cyril, closing his eyes as if ruminating on something.

Suddenly curious, Felix asked, "What sort of hallucinations were you having in the forest anyway?"

For a time, Cyril was silent, like he wasn't sure what to say. He was probably replaying the illusions he had seen on the backs of his eyelids.

Eventually, he slowly began to speak, eyes still shut. "...I saw a monster... A terrifyingly quiet, terrifyingly powerful monster... I doubt I'll ever forget the sight of it as long as I live."

* * *

After entrusting Cyril to Nero, Monica headed out of the forest, past the girls' dormitory, and toward the Serendia Academy school building. Ryn watched her impassively, head tilted so far to the side that she looked like a doll with a broken neck. This was apparently her way of indicating confusion.

"Aren't you returning to the dormitory?"

"...There's, um...something I wanted to, er, check on."

"Check on?" repeated Ryn.

Monica circled around to the back of the academy, then stopped in front of the rear gate. "...Lord Ashley's broach failed, um, because he was showered with powerful mana."

As a result, the magical broach, lacking a protective formula, had malfunctioned. Which begged the question: What was the source of the powerful mana to which Cyril had been exposed? It was logical to assume he'd come under some sort of magic-based attack.

"Lord Ashley was, um, very out of sorts earlier," she explained. "Rather than mana poisoning...his symptoms were closer to...the side effects of mental interference magecraft..."

Mental interference magecraft was a dangerous type of magic that was forbidden in most cases. It was possible to use it to perform simple brainwashing or fiddle with a person's memories to make them forget inconvenient truths, but its side effects included mental destabilization and intense mood swings.

Ryn had finally caught on to Monica's point. "In other words, the boy just now had recently been attacked by someone using mental interference magecraft, and that caused his magical broach to malfunction?"

"…Yes."

And if that was the case, then Monica had a pretty good idea of what had been going on at the academy.

Selma Karsh had dropped the flowerpot as revenge against Aaron's condemnation. But the truth about Aaron had been hidden from the students. They had been told only that he had voluntarily left school to recover from an illness.

Then why did Selma know the truth about Aaron's punishment? Logically, someone must have told her.

And the true criminal had used mental interference magecraft to work Selma into a frenzy—all in order to set her up as Aaron's accomplice.

Come to think of it, Aaron O'Brien's behavior also resembled the side effects of mental interference.

He'd claimed he'd had an accomplice—but also that he couldn't remember their name. Selma had claimed she was the one at fault for everything—but her words and actions had been incongruous. And now Cyril had been thrown into chaos and his mana out of control.

What if all three of them had been affected by a mind-altering spell?

Who had the means and the motive?

"…Miss Ryn, please hide for a moment."

"At once."

Ryn landed silently on a nearby tree branch, the skirt of her maid uniform fluttering.

As Monica was admiring the unique sense of lightness possessed by wind spirits, she caught sight of a figure next to the school building. She pulled back her hood and approached.

The figure, having just left the school building, caught sight of Monica and looked at her with suspicion.

"You're…Monica Norton, the new student, right?" he said,

fussily pushing up his spectacles. "And just what are you doing out so late at night?"

It was Monica's homeroom teacher and the adviser to the student council—Victor Thornlee. In his arms, he clutched a thick sheaf of paper as though it was very important. Monica stared fixedly at the papers, and Mr. Thornlee frowned.

"I'm sure curfew was quite some time ago. Going out this late without permission is grounds for suspension—"

"Those," said Monica, interrupting him, pointing at the papers Mr. Thornlee held. "Where are you...taking those?"

For a moment, Mr. Thornlee seemed embarrassed and at a loss for words. Behind his spectacles, his eyes shifted away ever so slightly.

"It's no use switching them with something else. I've memorized all the numbers in every document I've seen."

"Switch them...? What are you talking about?" asked Mr. Thornlee, his cheeks drawing back and his voice unnaturally high-pitched.

Until now, Monica's youthful face had always trembled in fear—but now, that fell away. It was just like when she'd been grappling with numbers in the student council room. A light shone, deep in her green eyes, as she peered at the documents in Mr. Thornlee's hands.

"The student council's accounting records have been a mess for quite some time now," she told him.

Every year, revenues and expenditures had failed to match. Ultimately, they'd been sloppily manipulated just to make the numbers line up. It had been a kind of tradition for the one in charge of accounting, the adviser, or whoever else to falsify them.

But Monica had noticed something during her review.

"Five years ago," she continued, "the way the numbers were falsified became more sophisticated. And what's more, the amounts of money began to get larger and larger."

After Aaron O'Brien had become accountant one year earlier, the amount of money had only further increased.

"Five years ago...was when you were appointed as adviser to the student council."

"What does that have to—?"

"Aaron O'Brien's accomplice in the embezzlement was you, Mr. Thornlee."

Rustle, rustle. The papers slid against one another as they fell from Mr. Thornlee's hands.

While Monica was distracted by this, Mr. Thornlee immediately closed the distance between them and grabbed her right wrist to keep her in place. He glared at Monica with hateful eyes and spat lowly, "For a failure of a student, you're awfully sharp."

"...Please let...go!"

Monica tried to shake him off, but the more she resisted, the angrier Mr. Thornlee got. His eyes as he looked down at her burned with a dense, concentrated hatred. "Magecraft research takes money, you know. And my research is so excellent...well, a mediocre girl like you would never be able to understand it, even if you tried for your entire life."

Mr. Thornlee gripped Monica's wrist so hard, he almost broke it, then used his other hand to cover Monica's face. She heard a soft chant. The formula was for...

Mental interference!

Once Mr. Thornlee was done chanting, a white light poured from his hand. "Burn this into your eyes—my perfect formula!"

Monica's vision went white.

Each of the particles of light was formed by tiny magical symbols. The flow of the light was itself one single magical formula. Monica stared right at it without averting her gaze.

"You saw nothing. And you'll forget about the numbers in the accounting records... Understand?"

Mr. Thornlee's suggestion was like a wedge pounded into a person's head. Attempting to go against that suggestion came with intense pain—like trying to rip the wedge back out.

But before it could gouge into Monica's mind, the wedge dissipated.

"...What...?"

Mr. Thornlee's magical formula collapsed, and the particles of light lost their glow. Monica looked up at him quietly; his eyes were wide. On that young, innocent face of hers was an expression of clear distaste.

Monica very rarely got angry about anything. No matter how much others made fun of her, no matter how many times they called her clumsy or stupid or incapable of doing things normal people could do, she could only hang her head, because they were right.

...But numbers and magecraft? Those were different.

The act of sullying perfect, beautiful equations and magical formulas was the one thing she could never bring herself to tolerate.

Mr. Thornlee's magical formula was just like the altered accounting books. It was a far cry from the perfect, beautiful formulas that Monica so loved.

"...This isn't...perfect in the slightest."

Mr. Thornlee glared at Monica, eyes bloodshot.

Normally, Monica would have cowered in fear and looked down with tears in her eyes. But Mr. Thornlee's unsightly formula had lit a fire in her heart. It had offended her pride as a mage.

She continued. "Mental interference spells require delicate mana control and a complicated, precise understanding of magical formulas. Yours is full of holes—far from...from perfect."

"Nonsense! It's perfect...!"

"...And yet, someone like me was able to block it?"

"Silence!"

Mr. Thornlee once again began to chant. His first formula was meant to seal a piece of a person's memories, but this chant was more vicious. It would utterly destroy the person's mind.

He raised his glowing-white palm. "A fool like you who cannot comprehend my excellence is better off as a mute doll!"

The moment his right hand touched Monica's head, she used her own mana to interfere with his magical formula. Such a move was extremely unconventional and possible only if the user had a very high level of skill. Monica managed it with ease.

First, she deciphered the formula Mr. Thornlee had woven, then dismantled it, pulling it apart like a mess of knotted string. That much was the same as when she'd nullified his first spell. The white light burst and dissipated, the glowing particles scattering around them.

But this time, after dismantling it, she kept the spell active and rewove it into something of her own—something more complex, more precise, and more beautiful. Something perfect.

The scattered particles of light began to swirl around her, as though each had a mind of its own, eventually forming shapes.

What is this? What's happening? thought Victor Thornlee, gasping in shock.

The light particles, whose shapes had previously been meaningless, had transformed into shining white butterflies. They left behind trails of glittering scales as they flew about in the darkness. It was a fantastic sight—beautiful enough to send a chill down one's spine.

However, anyone with even foundational knowledge of magecraft would be awestruck.

Each one of those butterflies…is a magical formula? And they're so incredibly advanced…

According to older magecraft texts, truly perfect mental interference formulas took on the form of butterflies. And right now, dancing before his eyes, were beautiful butterflies constructed only of magical formulas.

This was the perfected formula he'd never been able to reach, despite resorting to crime and pouring all his passion into the effort. And the one who had woven this formula so easily, without even chanting, was a little girl for whom he had felt nothing but disdain.

She was seedy-looking, certainly not suitable for this academy—and yet, not only had she seen through Thornlee's embezzlement, she'd negated his magecraft.

She'd demonstrated, as a mage, just how wide the gulf of ability was between them.

"It's not—it's not possible… It's just not… How could *you*, of all people…have such a perfect formula…and without chanting—?"

As he spoke, realization dawned.

Humans needed to chant to use magecraft. But there was just one person in this kingdom who had made the impossible possible.

A girl genius who had been selected as one of the Seven Sages two years ago at the young age of fifteen—as one of the pinnacles of magecraft.

The very genius who had unveiled a magical formula even more advanced than the one Thornlee had spent twenty years developing, shocking the magic world and tearing his own pride to shreds.

"You… You can't be the Silent—"

As if to interrupt him, the white butterflies began to stick to Thornlee's body, one after the other. When he tried to scrape them off, they covered his fingertips.

"Stop, no…! Stop this! Pleeease!"

The white butterflies covered both his shrieking mouth and his flailing limbs.

Finally, no longer able to move, Thornlee used his right eye, just barely showing through the coccoon of butterflies, to burn into his memory the image of the witch who had done this to him.

A small girl, skinny, with young features. Her green eyes, with a touch of brown in them, stared at him, emotionless and glittering like jewels in the light of the white butterflies.

And that monster in the form of a girl—the Silent Witch—spoke quietly and mercilessly.

"The spell will last for twenty-four hours. You'll dream of…"

* * *

Victor Thornlee was standing in a grassy field.

He knew these fields. They were the plains of his homeland.

But why was he in this empty countryside? He was too good to end up buried in a place like this.

Money. Not enough money. Magecraft research takes money. With money, I can do even better research. And then I can reclaim the dignity the Silent Witch stole from me…

To do that, he'd instigated the foolish Aaron O'Brien and dipped his hands in the vast wealth of Serendia Academy. And yet, that sharp-eyed prince had noticed Aaron's embezzlement.

That decorative prince—that mere puppet of Duke Clockford's!

And then Cyril Ashley, the vice president. He realized it was me embezzling the money. It was foolish of me to stop at erasing his memories. I should've brainwashed him. In fact, why don't I brainwash the president himself—the second prince? Then I'd be able to use the academy's money for anything I wished! I'd be set for life. Ah, why didn't I realize earlier how simple it was? Yes—I only need to make the second prince my puppet! And… Ah, yes, I must resume my research at once!

Triumphantly, Mr. Thornlee began to walk through the field. Then he noticed something in front of him. *Why, that's…*

"Oink."

A pig. *What is a pig doing in a place like this?*

Without thinking, he stopped and rubbed his eyes. Suddenly, there were two pigs. As he was wondering where they were coming from, even more started to appear.

Two became three, three became five, five became eight, eight became thirteen…

Before he knew it, he could see nothing but pigs around him.

Right, left, forward, backward—pigs, pigs, pigs, as far as the eye could see...

Eventually, he heard the sound of wagon wheels from afar. The pigs all began to shuffle toward the noise. Even then, their numbers never stopped increasing.

"Hey—what is—? No, stop! Stop, no, someone... Noooooooo!"

The world reflected in Mr. Thornlee's eyes was now buried, all the way to the horizon, in pigs.

As Mr. Thornlee shrieked, he was buried by the herd of pigs until, finally, he disappeared.

* * *

Monica squatted down next to Mr. Thornlee and held his head in her arms. He was foaming at the mouth, and his eyes had rolled back in his head.

"Wh-what should I do now? I...I went too far..."

When Mr. Thornlee had flaunted his imperfect formula in front of her, she hadn't been able to help getting worked up.

In the Kingdom of Ridill, the use of mental interference mage-craft was allowed only in examinations of those accused of serious crimes or in times of national emergency with the permission of the Mages Guild or the Seven Sages.

"...Ummm, I suppose I could say Mr. Thornlee committed a serious crime, since he was indirectly harming royalty? And members of the Seven Sages get a special exception, so this probably won't be considered a violation of the law. But... B-but what if it is...? Louis is going to be so mad at me... Wait, does that mean I'd be e-e-e-executed...?!"

As Monica muttered to herself, half in tears, Ryn came up behind her and tapped her on the back.

"I believe Lord Louis would say something like this." And then she put a hand to her chest and continued, "Anything goes as long as nobody knows."

Monica could practically see Louis Miller's handsome, malicious smile before her eyes. She wiped her tears on her sleeve as Ryn easily lifted up the white-eyed Mr. Thornlee.

"I shall deliver this man to Lord Louis. I believe he will tor— interrogate him, then dispose of him as necessary."

"Um, yes, thanks..."

Leaving aside Victor Thornlee's role in all the embezzlement, using a mental interference spell—a forbidden technique—without permission meant his disposal would fall to the Mages Guild.

There might be confusion at the academy over the sudden disappearance of a teacher, but Louis would do something about that, too. Probably. Monica breathed a sigh of relief.

On Ryn's shoulder, Mr. Thornlee was muttering to himself. "The pigs... The pigs..."

Confused, Ryn asked, "What sort of dream is he having at the moment, exactly?"

"Um, well..." Monica fidgeted with her fingers, then smiled just a little and said, "He's dreaming of a very beautiful sequence of numbers."

The Little Hand in His Memories

By the time Monica got back to her dorm room and finished writing a report to submit to Louis, dawn was breaking. When she'd lived in her mountain cabin, she had often pulled all-nighters. But now that she had been on a regular schedule for a little while, her head felt heavy with lack of sleep.

She walked to her classroom on wobbly legs, listened to Lana criticize her hair, and sat through the lesson, barely registering the buzz about Mr. Thornlee's sudden disappearance.

Her classes that day were a battle against drowsiness, and once they were over, she stifled a yawn and dragged her heavy legs over to the student council room.

When she got there, the place was empty. Apparently, she'd been the first to arrive. She did some light cleaning as Cyril had taught her, then some restocking. Finally, she opened the account books. But while looking at numbers would have normally perked her right up, today she found they just wouldn't stay in her head.

…Oh yeah. I used so much magecraft yesterday… I must need sugar.

Indifferent to food, Monica only ever ingested the bare minimum required. Her breakfast had been coffee and a piece of bread left over from dinner. She'd brought her own berries and water with her for lunch. Normally, she could make do with that, but when she used a lot of magecraft, it was no longer enough.

Spells required energy. Because of this, it was said that many mages were partial to sweets. Louis, for example, would always sneak baked goods made by his wife, Rosalie, into his pocket, occasionally stuffing them in Monica's mouth when she ran out of energy.

…I wonder if I have any snacks with me…?

Monica fished around in her pockets, but they were empty—she'd eaten all her berries for lunch. Telling herself that she only had to make it until her student council work was over, she eventually succumbed to drowsiness, and her face fell onto the desk.

While Monica was sleeping face-first in the accounting records, the door to the student council opened.

It was the student council's vice president, Cyril Ashley. He had arrived second after Monica.

When he noticed Monica sleeping at the desk, his eyebrows shot up. He opened his mouth to yell at her…but then stopped.

"……"

Cyril unconsciously quieted his footsteps as he approached the desk and looked down at Monica.

She was a thin, meager little girl. With her small, seedy-looking body, she certainly didn't appear seventeen. Her face was pale, and those eyes behind her long bangs were always looking down in hesitation. She was a plain, boring girl, the kind you could find anywhere—without even a shred of the elegance or beauty expected of nobles.

Cyril stared down at her right hand, still holding a feather pen. Most of the female students here had made-to-order gloves sporting lace, ribbon, and embroidery at the hems, but Monica's were stark white, unadorned. The fabric was a little loose on her, as though they didn't quite fit. That was how small her hands were—like a child's.

The scene from the night before flashed through Cyril's mind. The hand that had reached out for him after he'd fallen had been small like a child's—but it had had deep callouses that didn't match them. It had been the hand of someone who held a pen for hours each day.

Cyril gently removed the feather pen from Monica's hand and returned it to its stand. Her right hand fell limp, its fingers stretching lazily out across the desk. As if to measure how small her hands were, he covered her right hand with his own, then reached a finger toward the edge of her glove...

"Oh? Cyril, you're here already?"

At the sound of Felix's voice from behind him, Cyril immediately jumped back from the desk. "Your Royal Highness! This isn't what it looks like; this little brat is taking a nap in the sacred student council room, and I was just thinking of slapping her awake! Wake up already, you lazy runt!"

Cyril awkwardly raised his right hand and gave Monica a couple of smacks in the head. Monica raised her head off the desk, muttering to herself, her sleepy eyes going up to Cyril.

"...Lord Ashley?"

"H-hmph. Do you have any idea how silly you look right now? You are in the presence of His Royal Highness! Straighten up!"

Cyril grabbed her shoulder and shook. Monica continued to stare up at him...and eventually, she gave a crooked smile.

"...You're not cold... That's good..."

His deep blue eyes sprang open. He stopped shaking her and reached unconsciously for his broach. He worked his lips, trying to say something...when, just then, Felix reached in from beside him and pushed a cookie into Monica's mouth. She began to chew on it, still dozing. Felix pushed the cookie forward as it disappeared into her mouth, then eventually brought out another one and moved it close to her.

Monica, noticing the cookie pushing against her lips, started biting that one as well, still dozing.

"That's funny. She's mostly asleep, but her mouth is still moving."

"Uh, s-sir...?"

"Want to try, Cyril?"

The offer sounded like someone asking if he wanted to play with their pet. Cyril shook his head and said he'd rather not.

When Felix picked up a third cookie, Monica's head swayed to the side, and her eyes opened just a little. Appearing as if she'd just woken up, she rubbed her eyes, then muttered something incomprehensible under her breath.

Though Cyril had no way of knowing, Monica was currently writing a report in her dreams. Reports were one of Monica's least-favorite tasks. She never struggled to explain numbers or records but having to use sentences to explain a series of events was something she just wasn't very good at.

Where do I even start...? she groaned to herself, racking her brain. *I don't know...*

Meanwhile, Louis—who had appeared from out of nowhere— smiled at her. *Now then, my fellow Sage. You* do *know what you should write, don't you?*

If I don't write this report properly, she thought, *Louis will be mad at me. But where in the world am I even supposed to start?*

Oh, I know. There's one thing I definitely need to tell him...

Remembering something very important, Monica looked at the person in front of her and said, "...Congratulations on your wife's pregnancy."

"Who the hell are you talking about?!" yelled Cyril.

Felix put on a perfectly serious face and turned to him. "Cyril, who's the lucky lady? You better take responsibility for what you've done."

"What?! Sir?! That's not it! It's a misunderstanding. She's just asleep and speaking nonsense...!"

Cyril blushed, paled, and blushed again as he desperately tried to defend himself, not even realizing he was being teased.

All the while, Monica dozed on, trying to think of a good gift to present to the child of House Miller once they were born.

* * *

About a week after Monica had handed Mr. Thornlee over to Louis, his name appeared in the newspaper.

"Serendia Academy Teacher Arrested for Using Forbidden Magecraft!"

The newspaper was printed by a large company in the capital, so the incident became a topic of conversation even at Serendia Academy. Monica's classmates were especially shaken, since Mr. Thornlee had been their homeroom teacher.

"I can't believe Mr. Thornlee was doing such things! How scary… Monica, your right braid is coming loose."

"Huh?! Oh, oh no…!"

Monica, who had been braiding her own hair under Lana's supervision, quickly pressed her hand to the loosening braid. Her efforts, however, were in vain, and the whole braid fell apart in her hands. She'd have to do it all over again. It was easy enough to coarsely divide her hair in two and make a loose braid with it, but braids that went along the side of your head were quite a bit different.

"Uuugh… This is so hard…"

Lana had said it was cute when braids were gently loosened, but when Monica tried to do it, they just fell into shambles. Loosening them on purpose and having them naturally fall apart were entirely different things. Hanging her head glumly, Monica started over on her side braid.

"Come to think of it," remarked Lana, "the newspaper said the one who arrested Mr. Thornlee was one of the Seven Sages."

"Hu-what?!" The clump of hair fell from Monica's hand.

Lana sighed and rested her cheek on her hand without noticing the way Monica's face had tensed.

"It was Lord Louis Miller, the Barrier Mage. Have you heard of him? I saw him once at a party in the royal capital. He was a very stylish, handsome man."

"Ah, um, I—I—I—I, er, I s-see…"

Mages attended social events surprisingly frequently. That went double for the Seven Sages, who stood at the pinnacle of magecraft—some even called them the king's advisers. As such, they tended to attract attention wherever they appeared. Of course, Monica had never attended such a party.

"When it comes to the Seven Sages, the most famous are the Barrier Mage and the Starseer Witch, don't you think? Oh, and the Witch of Thorns and the Artillery Mage and—"

"E-excuse me!" squeaked Monica loudly and suddenly, earning a dubious look from Lana. Her face flushing bright red, Monica showed her the braid she'd just finished. "Th-this braid—I poured all my effort into making sure its ratios and angles were all perfect... H-how does it look?" she asked, glancing up at Lana.

Lana smiled and said, "It looks excellent."

* * *

The group that felt Mr. Thornlee's arrest most keenly—even more than Monica's class—was the student council. He had been their adviser, so it made perfect sense. And since it had come to light that he'd been involved in embezzling student council funds as well, faculty members had been in and out of the student council room all week. Things were about as busy as they could get.

"E-excuse me...," said Monica before nervously opening the door. Classes had ended, and she had come to visit the student council room.

There were no teachers inside—the only person there was Felix, sitting at the office desk in the back.

"There aren't, um, any teachers today, huh...?" asked Monica awkwardly.

Felix nodded serenely. "Yeah. It looks like things are settled for now. You've been working pretty hard for several days in a row, haven't you?"

"N-no, it really, um, wasn't that...that much..."

All the teachers rushing in and out had put her on edge, but being alone with the prince wasn't much different. Trying to make eye contact as little as possible, Monica got to work on today's documents.

Felix came up from behind and addressed her. "Oh, Lady Norton, your braid is coming loose."

"Huh?!"

Flustered, Monica put a hand to her head and felt her right braid falling apart.

"Wh-what...? I thought it was perfect this time..."

Despite the perfection with which she handled equations and magical formulas, she still had a lot of research to do when it came to braids. Her angles were perfect, but perhaps she'd started in a poor position. Or maybe she should have braided them more tightly... She groaned to herself, undoing her hair and re-braiding it, but she couldn't do very much without a comb.

"Shall I help you, Lady Norton?"

"N-no! I couldn't, um, possibly b-bother you with this...!" If Cyril was to find out that Felix had helped her, he'd yell at her again for being disrespectful.

Felix replied to Monica's flat refusal with a "huh" and narrowed his eyes meaningfully. "You know, Cyril or Lady Bridget will be here any moment. They're both very strict when it comes to appearances... Who could say what would happen if they found you like this?"

"...Ahhh...," Monica groaned.

"Want to run to the makeup room? Oh, but you'd probably be embarrassed if someone saw you in the hallway with that hair, wouldn't you?"

Monica groaned yet again. The more impatient she got, the more her hair slipped through her fingers.

Felix grinned, now sure of his victory, and held out a hand to her. "Come here. I won't tell Cyril or the others."

Monica nervously approached him. He had her sit down in his chair, and then he went behind her and started braiding her hair.

First, he straightened her hair with a comb, then quickly twisted a braid on the side of her head. Finally, he took the leftover hair and tied it all together with a ribbon. His motions were swift and smooth.

"There we are."

In less than two minutes, Felix had finished braiding Monica's hair. She timidly touched it—but even when she stroked it with her fingertip, it didn't feel like it would loosen.

"...That's amazing. You're very, um, good at this, sir."

"A prince must do everything perfectly."

I see, so princes must even learn how to braid hair. That seems more difficult than mastering magecraft or mathematics, thought Monica—an absurd notion—before suddenly realizing that she hadn't yet thanked Felix.

"Um! Er, th-thank you!"

"You're very welcome."

Once Felix had returned to his seat, the other student council members arrived one after the other. Monica hastily went back to her own chair as Elliott spoke, his expression weary.

"Ugh, I really hate this," he complained. "We've been cleaning up after Mr. Thornlee for *days*. And did you hear that he wasn't only embezzling student council funds? Apparently, he even used forbidden magecraft."

Neil answered him. "They say he was using the embezzled money to research magecraft, which is pretty expensive."

"Was he really that broke...? Where does Mr. Thornlee's family come from?" wondered Elliott.

"Luben," said Bridget simply.

When he heard this, Elliott's face filled with recognition. "Oh, I see. That's not a very wealthy area, and it suffered a lot of dragon-raids this year... Well, that's just what happens when you try to reach above your station. You reap what you sow." He smiled thinly, his drooping eyes narrowed.

Cyril was next to speak, documents in hand. "First former accountant Aaron O'Brien is caught embezzling, and then Mr. Thornlee, our adviser, is arrested. Trust in the student council is at an all-time low. We'll need to be extra careful with our work from here on out."

The room tensed at his words.

Felix looked over at Monica for some reason and said in a gentle voice, "Yes, Cyril's correct. And that's how it is, Lady Norton."

What does he mean, "that's how it is"? wondered Monica, straightening up. "Y-yes, sir."

"Would you mind," said Felix, "going around to all the club leaders and saying hello?"

"Saying...hello...?"

"Mm-hmm. Our new accountant still hasn't made her debut. It'll be very important for building up our trust with the club leaders." Felix thrust a list out toward Monica. It included the names of all the major clubs at Serendia Academy.

Unlike the other student council members, Monica had joined at a strange time, so naturally, nobody knew her yet. Because the accountant dealt with budgeting, she was bound to have especially frequent contact with club leaders. Accordingly, she needed to introduce herself.

Unfortunately, greeting and introducing herself for the first time was one of the things Monica was worst at. And now she had to do just that for more than twenty clubs.

Her face tensed and froze as Felix placed the list in her hand. Then, as if to encourage her, he covered her small hand with both of his and smiled softly.

"You'll be all right. You look incredibly cute today. Go introduce yourself. And have confidence."

Both his actions and words seemed aimed at encouraging her, but Monica could hear a voice in her head finishing his sentence: *I braided your hair myself, after all.*

Of course, this perfect prince would never say anything so condescending.

As she sat there petrified, the list was plucked from her hand. It was Cyril, who was now looking it over for himself.

"If you want to make it to all of these, you'll need to start immediately. I'll go with you."

Monica wasn't the only one surprised at that.

Elliott's droopy eyes widened as he looked at Cyril. "That's very kind of you. What's the occasion?"

"I've seen Monica Norton's work this past week, and I've decided that she's worthy of being introduced as our new accountant. That's all."

Monica gaped. Every time Cyril had seen her this past week, he'd scolded her for not being respectful enough to the prince, or for stammering too much, or for something similar. She'd been *sure* Cyril's constant anger was because he didn't think she was suitable for her position.

Cyril glared at her as she stood in shock.

"You heard me," he said. "Let's get going. Surely you won't say you *can't*, will you?"

Monica's mind went back to what had happened that night a week ago—to what Cyril had said just before passing out.

No such thing as can't...

I...I need to...live up to...

This young man wanted so badly to live up to someone's expectations that he'd tried to hold his head high until right before he'd lost consciousness. Even while mana was eating away at his entire body.

...She'd honestly thought it was incredible.

And such an incredible person was now acknowledging her as his accountant.

Monica played with her fingers and did her best to squeeze out her next words...

"Um...er... I-I-I'll do my besht!"

...only to stumble at the finish line. Her face went red, and she looked down.

Cyril's eyes widened just a little bit before he snorted proudly and quickly started off.

"Very well, then. Let's get moving, Accountant Norton!"

Accountant Norton. She'd never been called by her title before. The corners of Monica's lips twitched as she replied in the loudest voice she could manage:

"...Coming!"

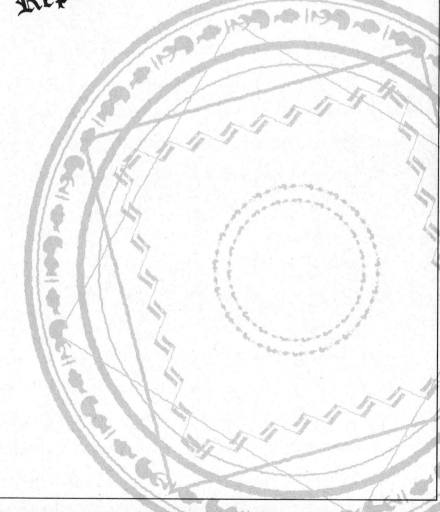

SECRET EPISODE

Report of the Silent Witch

To Louis,

Congratulations on your wife's pregnancy.

Regarding a gift for when the child is born, would an introductory book on mathematics be suitable?

If you have any particular mathematics books you are fond of, please let me know.

Regarding the mission, a lot has happened, and I've become the accountant of the student council.

The prince is also on the student council, so I think this will make it easier for me to guard him.

Lastly, regarding the string of incidents incited by Professor Victor Thornlee.

Mr. Thornlee conspired with the former student council accountant, Aaron O'Brien, to embezzle academy funds.

When it began to seem like he would be found out, he wiped Aaron's memory and attempted to place all the blame on Aaron's shoulders.

However, his mental interference formula was imperfect, and Aaron insisted to those around him that he'd had an accomplice.

When Mr. Thornlee realized others might find out that he was that accomplice, he used a mental interference spell on Aaron's fiancée, Selma Karsh, causing her to act recklessly.

Finally, Mr. Thornlee also used his mental interference mage-craft on Cyril Ashley, the vice president of the student council, then attempted to make off with the altered documents.

That was when I caught him in the act. I went a little too far. I apologize.

That concludes my report.

Adjusting to life at the academy has been difficult. But I'm going to keep trying for just a little bit longer.

The Silent Witch
Monica Everett

One week had passed since Monica had handed Victor Thornlee over to Louis.

Louis Miller, the Barrier Mage, had become very busy after that, passing Thornlee along to the Mages Guild, investigating further charges, and leaking information to the press.

At last, things had settled down, and Louis was reading over Monica's report again. No matter how many times he read it, he always finished with a sigh of exhaustion. He could see several sections crossed out and rewritten, so he knew she had done her best to choose her words properly... However...

"No matter how many times I read this, the only praiseworthy sentence in this report is the very first line."

"The first line?" repeated Ryn, who was standing behind Louis.

He snorted. "She gets good marks for offering her congratulations first. And yet, while her essays are so logical and well-formed, the girl's reports are an absolute mess!"

It was probably several times better than an oral report would have been, but for a report written by one of the Seven Sages, it was utterly deplorable.

"Being appointed to the student council in such a short time is a remarkable feat, and even I didn't predict it. That's the sort of thing that should have been written in detail...and yet, she glossed over it with a simple 'a lot has happened'? ...I know she has difficulty accepting praise, but this is a whole new level."

Joining the student council meant she'd won the trust of its president—the second prince. And she'd even succeeded in eliminating a shady character in his orbit. This was more than Louis had imagined—or could have hoped for.

...I had had my pupil infiltrate just to be sure, but to think she'd accomplish this much in this little time...

Louis read over the report one last time, then fed it to the flame of a candlestick. Once it had completely burned to ash, Louis pulled out another piece of paper.

This one was a document concerning Victor Thornlee's future. He'd be permanently stripped of his mage's qualifications—and it would probably be appropriate to follow that up with exile from the kingdom.

Apparently, his pride as a mage completely shattered, Thornlee was cooperating with the investigation without trouble. For some reason, however, he kept mumbling, "The pigs, the pigs," to himself, over and over.

"I wonder what sort of dream that girl showed Victor Thornlee," he mused.

"She claims it was a song about pigs belonging to a man named Mr. Sam," replied Ryn.

Louis frowned. "That's a song about pigs being sold off. A rather vulgar song for a girl who seems like she wouldn't hurt a fly..." He never could understand how Monica Everett's brain worked.

Sighing, he leaned back in his chair as Ryn set a cup of black tea in front of him. He opened up a drawer in his writing desk and took out his reserve of strawberry jam. Opening the lid, he poured it into the teacup, nice and thick, and mixed it around with a teaspoon. His wife always told him to eat sweets and drink alcohol in moderation, but after so much mental labor, there was nothing better than something sweet. He sipped at his black tea—which barely tasted like black tea anymore—a look of satisfaction on his face.

As he did, Ryn spoke. "I actually had something to ask of you, Lord Louis."

"What is it? If it's a silly question, I'll knock you flat," replied Louis as he took another sip, his eyes turning to look at her from behind his monocle.

But the spirit, insensitive as she was—or rather, she didn't have the same sort of sensitivities as a human in the first place—simply continued speaking at her own pace. "Why did you request that the Silent Witch guard the second prince?"

"I would ask your thoughts on that first, Rynzbelfeid."

Louis's contracted spirit had little expressiveness to speak of, but she had a habit of trying to act human by imitating those she read about in books. Without moving any part of her face, she brought a finger to her chin in a thinking gesture—then hit her palm with her fist as though she'd thought of something. "When you received this mission to guard the second prince, you worked day and night to create a magical item embedded with a defensive barrier. You gave it to the second prince, who then broke it, which you were very angry about."

"Yes, I seem to recall something like that."

"I believe that perhaps, in your rage, you vented your frustrations on the weak-willed Silent Witch to try and make yourself feel better."

Hearing her rude remark, one would doubt Louis was truly her master. But then, she didn't call Louis "Master" in the first place. This spirit had never had any intention of respecting him.

Louis returned his cup to the saucer and glared at her. "Just who do you think I am, exactly?"

"I hear from many different sources that you have a bankrupt personality and enjoy bullying the weak."

Another scathing criticism. Louis's handsome face twisted into a frown, and he continued in an exaggeratedly sorrowful voice. "Oh, how deplorable it is! I am *so* misunderstood."

"Misunderstood?" repeated Ryn flatly.

Louis slowly brought the corners of his lips up into a smile. The purplish-gray eye behind his monocle gleamed with belligerence. "Bullying the strong is much better sport than bullying the weak."

This was hardly a respectable motto. Not only was the idea alarming, but he hadn't even denied the comment about his personality.

Even presented with Louis's sinister grin, Ryn remained impassive, merely tilting her head to the side. "Lord Louis, it would seem to me that you are quite entertained with your tenacious tormenting of the Silent Witch. Does that not qualify as bullying the weak?"

"Her? *Weak?* Do you have any idea who you're talking about?"

"The Silent Witch spoke to me of how she was appointed to the Seven Sages from the waiting list."

The waiting list. Those three words made Louis's lips twist sardonically.

Two years ago, the Aquamancy Mage—a member of the Seven Sages at the time—had decided to retire, and so they had held a screening to decide who would be the replacement.

Originally, this meant only one person would be accepted. However, another one of the Seven Sages, who was advanced in age at the time, suddenly fell ill and was forced to retire. That meant they would need two.

The ones they'd chosen had been Louis Miller, the Barrier Mage, and Monica Everett, the Silent Witch.

The screening had consisted of an interview and practical combat trials where only magical attacks were permitted. Monica had hyperventilated during the interview out of nervousness; the way she'd passed out, eyes rolled back in her head, had been quite the rare disturbance. That was probably why she thought she had been appointed from the waiting list.

But none of the Sages serving on the screening committee had ever said a word about whether Louis or Monica was more talented.

"...She does seem to be convinced of it—but who can say if that's truly the case?"

True, Monica had committed a massive blunder during the interview. But she'd *still* been chosen as one of the Seven Sages. There must have been a pretty good reason for it.

Louis closed his eyes and recalled the combat test from two years ago. He was the former commander of the Magic Corps. He was considered an accomplished dragon slayer and was practically undefeated in battle. He had assumed a little girl with no combat experience could never hold a candle to him.

But then! That little girl—Monica! Wailing and crying, snot dripping from her nose, she had thrown out one absurdly powerful attack spell after the other, eventually completely shutting Louis out.

Louis was known as one of the more martial mages, but he couldn't so much as *scratch* this puny fifteen-year-old girl.

If a spell was particularly powerful, or wide ranging, or if it included any special effects, the chant would grow longer and longer in proportion.

And yet, the Silent Witch could easily wield magecraft that was high in power, wide in range, and chock-full of special effects without chanting at all.

Louis Miller had pride in his own genius. But if he was a genius, then Monica was…

"As the Barrier Mage Louis Miller, I can say this for certain. She is a monster."

Louis had firmly declared that this little girl, who never made eye contact and was always looking down nervously, was a monster.

After being shown the gap in their strength during the combat trials, he was not very happy to hear Monica insist she was selected only because she'd been on the waiting list.

The whole reason he'd dragged her along to slay the Black Dragon of Worgan was to instill some confidence in her. But after she'd defeated it, she'd fled right back to hole up in her mountain cabin.

You defeated me. If you put yourself down like that, then what does that make me?

Louis took another sip of his tea and narrowed his eyes. "I told my fellow Sage that should this mission fail, it could, at worst, mean execution—but I doubt the probability of that is very high."

"Why is that?"

"You see, His Majesty ordered me to secretly guard the second prince. But I couldn't believe that's what he really meant... I think the king's true intention is to keep an eye on the second prince in secret."

The second prince was a talented young man. He excelled at both book learning and swordsmanship, and he had gained the trust of nobles both within and without the kingdom with his strong diplomatic abilities—despite still being a student. His handsome features and soft smile—more from his mother than his father—charmed anyone who saw him. He mastered everything easily and had a superb understanding of how people felt and thought. Finally, he had his grandfather—Duke Clockford, a high noble with the most authority in the kingdom—at his back. Felix Arc Ridill had a *lot* going for him.

...And yet, he remains mysterious.

Louis always got an eerie feeling from the young man—it was like something disturbing lurked beneath that soft, friendly smile. But when Louis had attempted to pry into what was making him feel that way, Felix—with that soft smile of his—had passed it off and deflected.

"The second prince is quite the con artist. We won't be able to outwit him without thinking outside the box."

That was why Louis had chosen Monica as his collaborator—nothing about her added up, with her monstrous talents and shy personality.

"Like I said, I want to bully the strong, not the weak."

"In other words, you want to bully two strong people at once—the second prince and the Silent Witch."

Louis simply offered a handsome smile without confirming or denying.

Finally, he turned his back on her to signify that the conversation was over, before putting some more jam into the teacup, which was about half empty at this point. It was pretty much just jam now.

Ryn watched him impassively, then gave a firm nod. "I understand. I shall revise my personal estimation of you to *man with a morally bankrupt personality who enjoys bullying the strong.*"

"Revise the part about my 'morally bankrupt personality,' too, you failure of a maid!"

* * *

While Louis Miller was enjoying his jam-filled tea, the second prince in question, Felix Arc Ridill, was in his dorm room. He was also drinking some black tea, prepared for him by Wildianu. He, of course, wouldn't do anything so nonsensical as put an entire jar of jam into it. No, the prince melted only a single cube of sugar into his cup.

"I suppose we've mostly finished sorting out the Thornlee affair," he said calmly as he drank. "And it seems the introductions to the club leaders have gone over without issue as well."

Although Monica was extremely shy, she had managed to greet everyone before the day was over, then return to the student council room with Cyril. Felix smiled a little—as he'd thought, leaving Monica in Cyril's hands had been the correct choice.

Despite how he sometimes seemed, Cyril was a helpful person who was good at taking care of others. Most importantly, he was able to fairly judge a person on their abilities rather than just their social standing. The trouble was that he was so loyal to Felix that he went a little out of control sometimes.

"It seems neither Elliott nor Lady Bridget has accepted Lady Norton just yet, but... Well, the new student council shouldn't have any problems doing its job, at least."

And that meant things were just about wrapped up.

As Felix finished his tea, Wildianu—who had transformed into a servant—offered a modest comment. "I am somewhat surprised. I had thought Duke Clockford would criticize you."

"That's true. When something goes wrong at the academy, it means my management has fallen short."

Duke Clockford was Felix's maternal grandfather and one of the most influential people in the kingdom. He was also, essentially, the ruler of Serendia Academy. Even Felix, the second prince, couldn't defy him. That was why some people called Felix a puppet prince or Duke Clockford's lapdog.

"But this time," he continued, "it's likely the duke can't be cross with me. After all, he was the one who originally hired Mr. Thornlee and ordered me to select the former accountant O'Brien for the student council." The Barrier Mage—the one who had arrested Mr. Thornlee—was surely in Duke Clockford's bad books now. "Still, it is a shame. I would have liked to hand down judgment personally on Mr. Thornlee like I did for Aaron O'Brien."

"Were you aware of his involvement in the embezzling?"

"Yeah. I was thinking he would give himself away soon, but it looks like someone beat me to the chase. The Barrier Mage has been sticking his nose into my business lately, after all. He probably caught on to Mr. Thornlee's crimes in the process."

His voice cold, Felix took a small broach from his pocket. It was a gorgeous broach, once embedded with a large sapphire—but the sapphire inside was cracked and coming loose from its gallery. Felix plucked the cracked sapphire up and held it to the light.

When he focused, he could see magical formulas engraved in the blue jewel. This broach had been imbued with magecraft; it was what they called a magical item. Louis Miller, the Barrier Mage, had told the king it was to protect him, and the king had passed it to Felix. And it had indeed been imbued with a defensive barrier that would activate if he came under attack.

But that wasn't the only effect it had been imbued with.

"As long as I wear this broach, the Barrier Mage knows exactly where I am. It has a formula embedded within it to tell him."

"...Yes."

That was why Felix had given the broach to Wildianu to destroy as soon as he'd received it. To everyone else, Felix appeared an amateur when it came to magic. Even Louis probably hadn't expected him to notice the surveillance tracking formula inside it.

"The Barrier Mage is watching me... But is it at the behest of the first prince's faction or His Majesty?"

Either way, he knew it would behoove him to act with care for the time being. He leaned back on the sofa and gave a long sigh.

"Well, if they were going to assign one of the Seven Sages to monitor me, there's someone else I would have preferred."

"...And who might that be?" asked Wildianu dubiously.

Felix's face broke into an enchanting smile. "The hero of our kingdom—the one who defeated the Black Dragon of Worgan as well as an entire horde of pterodragons in one fell swoop. The only person in the world who can use unchanted magecraft, the kind of genius who only appears once in a millennium..."

As he spoke, his voice grew more passionate, bringing a touch of scarlet to his handsome white cheeks. He seemed almost entranced, as though he was speaking of someone very dear to him.

"The Silent Witch—Lady Everett."

Characters So Far

Characters

Monica Everett

The Silent Witch, one of the Seven Sages. The only one in the world capable of using unchanted magecraft.

To protect the second prince, she enrolls at Serendia Academy, calling herself Monica Norton. Extremely shy.

Louis Miller

The Barrier Mage, one of the Seven Sages. Became a Sage alongside Monica. Newlywed.

A handsome man with a feminine face but a fighter at heart. He holds the second-highest record for solo dragon slaying. A happy feller soon to be a father.

Nero

A black cat who serves as Monica's familiar. An avid reader. Loves adventure novels but has recently started getting into romance novels as well. Can do a variety of tricks, such as sensing mana, transforming into a human, and striking sexy poses.

Rynzbelfeid

A high wind spirit contracted to Louis.

Does not particularly care for or respect her master. She has read many books in order to learn about humans, but her vocabulary and common sense are rather skewed.

Felix Arc Ridill

Second prince of the Kingdom of Ridill. President of Serendia Academy's student council.

Has excellent grades as well as diplomatic achievements under his belt. A well-rounded boy who excels at everything.

His face and body adhere to the golden ratio (according to Monica).

Elliott Howard

Son of Count Dasvy. One of the student council secretaries.

A contrarian who clings to the social hierarchy. Especially good at chess.

The representative "droopy-eyed" character in this story.

Cyril Ashley

Foster son of Marquess Highown. Vice president of the student council.

Specializes in ice magecraft. Has a condition called mana hyperabsorption. Reveres Felix.

Generally polite to women, except for those who are rude to Felix.

Bridget Greyham

Daughter of Marquess Shaleberry. One of the student council secretaries.

Hails from a family of diplomats and talented at languages. A beautiful noble girl said to be the most fitting to become Felix's fiancée. Likes dogs more than cats.

Neil Clay Maywood

Son of Baron Maywood. Officer of general affairs of the student council.

Good-natured, mild-mannered, and friendly, but tends to get swept away by others. His uniform was tailored in the expectation that he'd get taller, but he still hasn't filled it out.

Isabelle Norton

Daughter of Count Kerbeck. A huge fan of the Silent Witch and Monica's collaborator on her mission.

Tirelessly working to perfect her role as villainess. The sharpness of her laughter is in a class of its own.

Lana Colette

Daughter of Baron Colette and Monica's classmate. Up on the latest trends and loves fashion. Her father is very wealthy. In the future, she wants to open a trading company like her father.

Afterword

Thank you very much for purchasing *Secrets of the Silent Witch*.

The web version of this book comprises sixteen parts in all, and I wrote it imagining it would be a single story from chapter one through chapter sixteen.

With the novelization of the story, the first book will contain chapters one through three.

However, this volume would have lacked the excitement and coherence to stand alone if I'd kept the web version as it was.

So I thought hard about what edits and retouches to make so that this volume could be enjoyed as a single book.

I hope both those who are reading the story for the first time and those who have already read the web version enjoy this novelization of *Secrets of the Silent Witch*.

The retouching work was a battle against character limits.

Writing is so incredibly fun for me. Keeping my eye on the remaining character count, I'd find myself getting greedy—I'd want to write this, and that, and also this other thing, and even more of something else. It was honestly a lot of fun.

If I wanted to, I could easily write plenty of scenes about Monica's daily life in her mountain cabin. (But then she'd never make it to the academy.)

And then I'd write pages and pages of Lady Isabelle praising her elder sister. (But then they'd never make it to the academy.)

Just the scene where Louis Miller rubs in his boundless love for his new wife in front of Monica threatened to fill up half the book. (But then they'd never… Well, you get the point.)

…I think the biggest problem to tackle was how to best set the pace leading up to their arrival at the academy.

During the retouching, I revised the web version to be kinder to Monica in general.

This was because the editor, a very kind person, is fond of Monica and always calls her cute.

If Monica should ever get into an even more terrible situation than in the web version, please think to yourself, *The writer must have insisted on this.*

The editor is very kind to Monica. The writer is the one who is unkind to her.

Finally, thank you for the exquisite, warm, beautiful illustrations, Nanna Fujimi-sensei. I looked at them many times over while writing and always grinned and chuckled to myself.

I'd also like to thank everyone at Kadokawa for working so hard on the novelization, as well as my editor, who gave me—someone who barely knows right from left—a lot of good advice.

And I'd like to once again thank everyone who has read this story, as well as anyone who has even been remotely involved with my creating it.

It's thanks to the efforts of many, many people that this story was able to reach the world in book format.

I cannot thank you all enough.

I'm also incredibly grateful that this book will be getting a continuation. I'll continue to do my best with my writing, so please look forward to the next volume as well.

Matsuri Isora

HAVE YOU BEEN TURNED ON TO LIGHT NOVELS YET?

86—EIGHTY-SIX, VOL. 1-10

In truth, there is no such thing as a bloodless war. Beyond the fortified walls protecting the eighty-five Republic Sectors lies the "nonexistent" Eighty-Sixth Sector. The young men and women of this forsaken land are branded the Eighty-Six and, stripped of their humanity, pilot "unmanned" weapons into battle...

Manga adaptation available now!

WOLF & PARCHMENT, VOL. 1-6

The young man Col dreams of one day joining the holy clergy and departs on a journey from the bathhouse, Spice and Wolf. Winfiel Kingdom's prince has invited him to help correct the sins of the Church. But as his travels begin, Col discovers in his luggage a young girl with a wolf's ears and tail named Myuri who stowed away for the ride!

Manga adaptation available now!

SOLO LEVELING, VOL. 1-4

E-rank hunter Jinwoo Sung has no money, no talent, and no prospects to speak of—and apparently, no luck, either! When he enters a hidden double dungeon one fateful day, he's abandoned by his party and left to die at the hands of some of the most horrific monsters he's ever encountered.

Comic adaptation available now!